200 HARLEY STREET

Welcome to the luxurious premises of
the exclusive Hunter Clinic, world renowned
in plastic and reconstructive surgery,
set right on Harley Street, the centre of
elite clinical excellence, in the heart of
London's glittering West End!

Owned by two very different brothers,
Leo and Ethan Hunter, the Hunter Clinic
undertakes both cosmetic and reconstructive
surgery. Playboy Leo handles the rich and
famous clients, enjoying the red carpet
glamour of London's A-list social scene,
while brooding ex-army doc Ethan
focuses his time on his passion—
transforming the lives of injured war heroes
and civilian casualties of war.

Emotion and drama abound against the
backdrop of one of Europe's most glamorous
cities, as Leo and Ethan work
through their tensions and find women
who will change their lives for ever!

200 HARLEY STREET

*Glamour, intensity, desire—the lives and loves
of London's hottest team of surgeons!*

Dear Reader

I've always loved reading continuity stories, so it was a thrill to be asked to write one and an honour to be in the company of the other wonderful authors who have contributed to this series.

From the moment he came alive on the page for me I knew that Edward was going to be a challenge. He's one of those people who'll shine at whatever he turns his hand to. He might not be much of a team player, but give him a problem and he'll come up with a brilliant and imaginative solution. He has his work, his books and his music, and seems to want nothing and no one else. What can you give a man like that?

Well, you can give him Charlotte. Charlotte might not always understand the complexities of Edward's thought processes, but she understands people. And as she gets to know Edward it becomes obvious that there's something missing in his well-ordered life. But she and her son have been hurt once already, and the one thing that Edward needs is the thing that Charlotte has promised herself she'll never give.

I hope that you enjoy Edward and Charlotte's story. I'm always delighted to hear from readers, and you can contact me via my website at www.annieclaydon.com

Annie x

Praise for
Annie Claydon:

'Well-written brilliant characters—I have never been disappointed by a book written by Annie Claydon.'
—*GoodReads* on
THE REBEL AND MISS JONES

3 8014 05262 6493

200 HARLEY STREET: THE ENIGMATIC SURGEON

BY
ANNIE CLAYDON

First published in Great Britain 2014
by Mills & Boon, an imprint of Harlequin (UK) Limited,
Large Print edition 2014
Eton House, 18-24 Paradise Road,
Richmond, Surrey, TW9 1SR

© 2014 Harlequin Books S.A.

Special thanks and acknowledgement are given to Annie Claydon for her contribution to the *200 Harley Street* series

ISBN: 978-0-263-23915-7

Printed and bound in Great Britain
by CPI Antony Rowe, Chippenham, Wiltshire

Cursed from an early age with a poor sense of direction and a propensity to read, **Annie Claydon** spent much of her childhood lost in books. After completing her degree in English Literature she indulged her love of romantic fiction and spent a long, hot summer writing a book of her own. It was duly rejected and life took over. A series of U-turns led in the unlikely direction of a career in computing and information technology, but the lure of the printed page proved too much to bear, and she now has the perfect outlet for the stories which have always run through her head, writing Medical Romance™ for Mills & Boon®. Living in London—a city where getting lost can be a joy—she has no regrets for having taken her time in working her way back to the place that she started from.

Recent titles by Annie Claydon:

ONCE UPON A CHRISTMAS NIGHT…
RE-AWAKENING HIS SHY NURSE
THE REBEL AND MISS JONES
THE DOCTOR MEETS HER MATCH
DOCTOR ON HER DOORSTEP
ALL SHE WANTS FOR CHRISTMAS

These books are also available in eBook format from www.millsandboon.co.uk

Dedication

To the ladies who lunch: Yve, Nicky and Vicki.

200 HARLEY STREET

Glamour, intensity, desire—the lives and loves of London's hottest team of surgeons!

For the next four months enter the world of London's elite surgeons as they transform the lives of their patients and find love amidst a sea of passions and tensions…!

Renowned plastic surgeon and legendary playboy Leo Hunter can't resist the challenge of unbuttoning the intriguing new head nurse, Lizzie Birch!
200 HARLEY STREET: SURGEON IN A TUX
by Carol Marinelli

Glamorous Head of PR Lexi Robbins is determined to make gruff, grieving and super-sexy Scottish surgeon Iain MacKenzie her Hunter Clinic star!
200 HARLEY STREET: GIRL FROM THE RED CARPET
by Scarlet Wilson

Top-notch surgeons and estranged spouses Rafael and Abbie de Luca find being forced to work together again tough as their passion is as incendiary as ever!
200 HARLEY STREET: THE PROUD ITALIAN
by Alison Roberts

One night with his new colleague, surgeon Grace Turner, sees former Hollywood plastic surgeon Mitchell Cooper daring to live again…
200 HARLEY STREET: AMERICAN SURGEON IN LONDON
by Lynne Marshall

Injured war hero Prince Marco meets physical therapist Becca Anderson—the woman he once shared a magical *forbidden* summer romance with long ago…
200 HARLEY STREET: THE SOLDIER PRINCE
by Kate Hardy

When genius micro-surgeon Edward North meets single mum Nurse Charlotte King she opens his eyes to a whole new world…
200 HARLEY STREET: THE ENIGMATIC SURGEON
by Annie Claydon

Junior surgeon Kara must work with hot-shot Irish surgeon Declan Underwood—the man she kissed at the hospital ball!
200 HARLEY STREET: THE SHAMELESS MAVERICK
by Louisa George

Brilliant charity surgeon Olivia Fairchild faces the man who once broke her heart—damaged ex-soldier Ethan Hunter. Yet she's unprepared for his haunted eyes and the shock of his sensual touch…!
200 HARLEY STREET: THE TORTURED HERO by Amy Andrews

Experience glamour, tension, heartbreak and emotion at 200 HARLEY STREET in this new eight-book continuity from Mills & Boon® Medical Romance™

These books are also available in eBook format and in two 200 HARLEY STREET collection bundles from www.millsandboon.co.uk

CHAPTER ONE

'SO WHICH IS it, then?'

'Eh?' Charlotte King was busy trying not to notice that Edward North was currently going through his pockets to find the key to his office, and she had lost the thread of the conversation that was going on around the nurses' station.

'Which do you think? Secret love-life, or no love-life?' Paula craned across the desk to get a better view. 'Wonder if he needs a hand with that?'

Charlotte swallowed a laugh. 'What? You know where he's left his keys?'

'No. But I'm really good at finding things.' Paula's smile left no doubt that she was contemplating a thorough investigation and possibly a body search.

'Too late. He's got them.' Allie grinned at Paula. 'And I reckon he's got a secret mistress somewhere.'

'When does he get to see her? In between here

and the hospital, I'd be surprised if he has much time for anything else.'

'He has time to swim.' Allie's blue eyes flashed mischievously.

'Yeah?' Paula's attention was on Allie now.

'Mmm-hmm. I left my trainers downstairs in the gym the other day and went to fetch them after work. He was in the pool, doing laps.'

'Hmm. Perhaps I'll go buy myself a swimming costume. Common interests can be very important in a relationship.'

'So you've thought this through, then?' Charlotte wished that Paula and Allie would keep their voices down. Not that the nurses were in any danger of being heard. It was difficult enough to get Edward's attention even when he was supposed to be listening to you. It just seemed somehow wrong to be talking like this.

'Who hasn't? I reckon he just needs a good woman. And I'll apply for the position if no one else is interested.'

Allie laughed. 'Steady, Paula. Remember there's a queue and I'm in it. Charlotte, too, eh?'

Charlotte considered the prospect. She couldn't get away with a lie that big. 'Yeah, okay. Just to keep you two company, though. I don't have time for dating.'

Or the money. Or the inclination, most of the time. Apart from when Edward… Her gaze wandered over to the glazed wall of his office. He was behind his desk now, deep in thought, a stack of papers and books in front of him.

'Yeah, right.' Paula was laughing now. 'Guess we could share him around.'

Oh, no. Edward wasn't for sharing. He was for being loved, nurtured by one woman, not passed around like a beautifully wrapped, enormously sexy parcel. He looked up, as if somehow the thought had penetrated the walls of his office, his eyes suddenly focussing in Charlotte's direction.

She could feel the flush spreading up from the back of her neck to her cheeks. Edward might be for one woman, but that woman definitely wasn't her.

Charlotte turned, trying to pretend that he hadn't just caught her staring at him. 'I'll leave you to do that. I've got to do my last ward round and my friend is bringing Isaac here soon.'

'Really?' Paula always made a particular fuss of Isaac. 'What do we owe that pleasure to?'

'There's no school today and my friend's been

looking after him. Lucy's got a date tonight so she's dropping him off here before she goes on to hit the town. If you see them, will you get them to wait here?'

Paula nodded. 'Sure thing. Take your time.'

Edward North had just got to the complex part. Not that tomorrow's microsurgery wasn't all complex, but this particular section was intricate in the extreme. Running through it in his head was his preferred method of preparation, and the swimming pool in the basement of the Hunter Clinic his preferred place. Working his body seemed to free his mind, but he couldn't be assured of solitude until the clinic was closed for the day, so his office was going to have to do.

'No. Not like that…' He shook his head, muttering in disgust at his own ineptitude. He'd have to start over now. Or at least from the last set of microscopic sutures. Edward took a breath, cleared his mind, and…

The image that floated into his mind was nothing like the one he was concentrating on building. Pale chestnut hair, bound in a tight knot at the back of her head. Light brown eyes. He couldn't see the flecks of gold from this distance, but he knew that they were there. Somehow Charlotte's eyes had impressed themselves on his consciousness when he had difficulty in recalling the names, let alone the eye colour, of most of the rest of the nursing staff.

She'd looked away, then. Blushing.

The exact mechanics of that particular form of vasodilation was child's play alongside the complexities of its causes. Most things were. Edward closed his eyes, cleared his mind, and went back to the matter in hand.

Lucy was already standing at the nurses' station when Charlotte returned from her ward round.

'Hey, Lucy, you look nice. I won't be a minute. I've just got to pick up my coat.' Charlotte looked around. Just one glimpse of her son after a long day was always enough to lift her spirits.

'Sure. Why don't you leave Isaac here with me?'

'Isn't he with you?'

'No. He ran ahead up the stairs. I called after him to wait for you here...'

For one split second the two women stared at each other. Charlotte almost choked as something squeezed tight around her heart, and then instinct and the sure knowledge that she needed to move *now* took over.

'Go downstairs, Lucy. Make sure he's not slipped out of the building. I'll look for him here.'

She glanced over in the direction of Edward's office. The view inside was partially obscured by a long, low cabinet, running the length of the glass wall and designed to keep the mess of books and other artefacts under some semblance of control, but she could see that he was no longer sitting at his desk. Not that he'd probably notice if a whole horde of five-year-olds started roaming the corridors, but he'd been the only one there and beggars couldn't be choosers.

Isaac shouldn't have gone into any of the treatment rooms. He knew not to do that. All the same she looked, trying not to panic, trying not to cry. Allie hadn't seen him and neither had Paula. She opened every cupboard, every locked door, just in case. And each time her baby wasn't there the agitation in the pit of her stomach grew.

'The receptionist says that he can't havΔ9
e got out of the building. He would have had to have either opened one of the back doors, and they're all alarmed, or gone straight past her.' Lucy arrived back upstairs, red and breathless.

That was something, at least. Mind you, there was plenty of trouble right here that a five-year-old could get into. The swimming pool...Charlotte remembered the swimming pool in the basement and felt suddenly sick.

'I'll call Security...' She grabbed for the phone and then dropped it. Either she was hearing things, or...

Isaac laughed again. That was definitely not a hallucination.

Lucy had heard it, too. 'Where is he?' Lucy looked around wildly.

Another laugh. This time deep, round and rich. The kind of laugh that Edward might have, only Charlotte didn't think she'd ever heard him laugh. Wordlessly she swung round and marched towards the door of Edward's office, opening it without bothering to knock.

For a moment, in the relief of seeing that Isaac was safe, she didn't register the scene in front of her. Somehow she noticed that Isaac's favourite toy, the blue bunny that he carried with him everywhere, was sitting in Edward's black leather chair, and that Edward was on the floor.

'Isaac!' Charlotte gulped out his name. 'What are you doing?'

Her son looked up at her. Innocent blue eyes and dark blond hair framed the sweet smile which never failed to dissolve her anger and dispel her fears.

'Hi, Mum. I'm making water.' He picked up a small red ball from the box in front of him. 'Look, you take one red one. That's…'

'Um…oxygen.' Edward got to his feet quickly, facing Charlotte with a slightly abashed air. 'So you're Isaac's mother?'

'Yes.' She ducked around Edward. She could deal with him later. 'Isaac, come here, please.'

'But, Mum, I haven't shown you. Look…'

'We mustn't bother Mr North any more, sweetie. Where did you get that from?' She looked at the molecule model kit in front of him on the floor. It looked like a great toy and she wished she could afford something like it for Isaac, even if he was a bit young for it at the moment.

'It's Edward's.' Isaac shot a pleading look up at his new friend, who ignored him completely and sat down in his chair, remembering just in time to pull the blue bunny out from under him before it got squashed. He proffered it to Isaac and when he didn't show any inclination to take it propped it up against the phone.

It had been a long week, and Charlotte had just about had enough. You could only take so many small crises, each one popping up hard on the heels of the last, before life became one big crisis.

'Then put everything back in the box and say thank you to Edward. We've got to get home.' Hopefully she could get out of here before the temptation to tear Edward off a strip became too great. Didn't he realise that someone would be looking for the stray five-year-old who had wandered into his office?

Isaac shot her a look which left her in no doubt that he wasn't in agreement with that decision, but complied anyway. One down, one to go. Charlotte turned to Edward, who was arranging the blue bunny into a crossed-legs, hands-behind-the-head posture which gave the impression that he was leaning back against the phone, sunbathing.

'I'm sorry he...interrupted you. We'll be going home...'

The sheer force of his gaze stopped her. Thoughtful. Intensely blue. And at this moment tainted with an uncertainty that was unlike Edward.

'Were you looking for him?'

'Yes. But it's all right, he's here...' Charlotte

just wanted to hug Isaac. As soon as she got out of Edward's office that was the first thing she planned to do.

'I should have let you know he was here.'

He'd recovered himself now. Whatever emotion he did or didn't feel was locked away somewhere, no one's business but his own.

'That's okay. I've found him now...' She was shaking. So tired that she was almost in tears. All she wanted to do was get home. 'Isaac, will you give Edward the box back, please?'

Isaac seemed to have got over his disappointment and carefully collected up the box and laid it on Edward's desk. 'Thank you.'

'You're welcome.' Edward gave Isaac a guarded half-smile and a little formal nod and her son copied the expression in return. 'Don't forget... What's his name?'

'Stinky.'

Edward raised one eyebrow. 'Well, don't forget Stinky, then.'

He looked up at Charlotte and she tried for a smile.

'Will you stay a moment, please, Charlotte?'

This was the last thing she needed right now. She knew that Isaac shouldn't have been running around the clinic on his own. Edward didn't need to tell her that, and it went without saying that it wouldn't happen again. 'Isaac, will you go and sit with Lucy, please? Just for a minute.' She pointed to the patients' seating area outside.

'Here.' Edward leaned forward, towards the boy, proffering a handful of change. 'Get something for yourself and Lucy from the vending machine. D'you think Stinky wants anything?'

'No, he doesn't. He's not a real rabbit, you know.'

'Of course not. Well, something for you and Lucy then...'

Charlotte was about to stop Isaac from taking the money, but Edward had already put a selection of coins into his hand and Isaac was halfway towards the door. At least he remembered to thank Edward. She straightened herself and prepared for the dressing down that was coming.

'I'm sorry, Charlotte.'

'Eh...?'

'You must have been worried when you couldn't find Isaac.'

Worried? Frantic, more like. 'I...I'm sorry he bothered you.'

'He was no trouble. He seems to like molecules...' Edward almost smiled and then thought better of it. Too bad. In that brief moment his eyes had seemed bluer, and his dark good looks less brooding.

'He's only five. He likes putting things together and taking them apart again...' The rush of relief at finding Isaac had left her feeling like a limp dishcloth. And now this. Instinctively Charlotte put one hand to her brow, as if to shade herself from the intensity of those blue eyes which seemed to hold so much that was unsaid.

'Hey. What's this?'

He was on his feet, his hands on her shoulders. Edward had the worst timing of any man she'd ever known, bar none. Of all the times to choose to be kind, this was the one most likely to reduce her to tears.

'Nothing. It's nothing. I'm okay.' She tried to avoid his gaze.

'Clearly you're not.'

There was a note of tenderness in his voice that she hadn't heard before. Something warm about the arm which wound around her shoulder. Something about his scent that made her instinctively sink into him, even though she knew that this was probably one of the worst ideas she'd ever had in her life.

Under the crisp white shirt there was some serious musculature. Strong arms, and a flat, hard stomach. For the second time in the last few minutes the swimming pool flashed into Charlotte's head, but this time the image was considerably more inviting.

'I'm okay...' Charlotte thought about pushing him away and then decided that putting her hands anywhere near him would be far too much of a temptation. 'Really. I'm fine.'

He seemed to feel it, too. He stepped back quickly, almost as if she'd burnt him, and turned towards his desk. 'If there's anything that's bothering you, you should let someone know.' He thought for a moment, obviously considering himself an unlikely candidate for any kind of emotional disclosure. 'Lizzie, perhaps...I'm sure she'd be able to do...whatever's needed.'

Edward had switched back into professional mode and the relief was almost palpable. 'No. There's nothing. I just had a bit of a scare when I couldn't find Isaac...' She bit her words back. Nothing like blaming the very person who had just tried to help her.

'I'm sorry. It won't happen again.'

That was supposed to be *her* line. She smiled

up at him, wishing that she could smooth some of the creases on his brow. 'It's okay. He's safe, and that's all that matters. I'm sorry he disturbed you. He knows he mustn't wander around here.'

'That's all right. It was nice to talk to him.' He gestured stiffly towards the molecule model kit. 'His approach is refreshingly creative, compared with most.'

Was that a joke? It was difficult to tell with Edward, but the possibility intrigued Charlotte. She could see Lucy and Isaac out of the corner of her eye, settling themselves down on the sofa with their drinks. They'd be at least another five minutes, and hadn't Paula always said that Charlotte only needed five minutes to get anyone to open up?

'What's it for? If you don't mind my asking?'

'You can use it for anything. I'm thinking of DNA sequencing.' The way he brushed off the question almost made her believe that everyone had a model of a DNA sequence somewhere in their office.

'Ah. Right. Anyone in particular?'

'Mine, actually. Just a snippet of it, of course. But don't you think there's something rather inter-

esting about actually being able to look at something that's the very basis of your own make-up?'

'I'd never really thought about it.' Now he mentioned it, there was. There was an obscure symmetry about the concept that made her smile, even
if she didn't properly understand it.

'You should. It would be interesting for Isaac...'
He narrowed his eyes. 'Perhaps when he's a bit
older.'

'Yes, I think so. Is that all?' She should go now.
She'd managed to stem her tears for the moment,
but who knew how long that particular dam was
going to hold? Hopefully until after Isaac was
safely tucked up in bed.

'Are you going home? I'm going your way. I'll
give you a lift. The buses are horrible at this time
of day—' He broke off, as if he'd let something
slip that he shouldn't.

How did he know she took the bus home? And
how did he know which way she went? Charlotte
stared at him.

'I've seen you waiting at the two-three-nine bus
stop. And the two-three-nine goes almost directly
along my route home. Of course you could be
catching the number thirteen, but most people
who do that walk down to the Oxford Circus stop,

so they can get a seat—' He broke off again, obviously wondering whether that was too much
information.

'Right. Next time I want to know which bus to
take, I'll know who to ask.' She grinned at him.
'But it's okay, really. You must still have work to
do and we'll be going in a minute.'

He shrugged. 'I was operating at six this morning, I should have been gone hours ago. And...
You look tired.'

Perhaps Edward noticed more than everyone
thought.

There was no perhaps about it. He clearly did.
Somewhere inside a smile formed at the thought
that some of those things were connected with her.

'We...we can't. Isaac needs a proper car seat...'
It was a pity. The buses were always packed on
a Friday evening and she could have done with a
ride home.

'No problem. I have one fitted in my car.'

Something told Charlotte that Edward had
worked all of this through before he'd even made
the offer. The complex equation balanced two
shopping bags, one child and an indeterminate
number of full buses, crawling through the traffic, against one child seat, a comfortable car and

a lift home. He probably already knew what she was about to say.

She smiled, wondering whether he'd factored that in or not. 'Okay. If it's no trouble. Thanks.'

CHAPTER TWO

EDWARD GAVE NO explanation for the brand-new child's car seat when he opened the back door of his sleek dark blue car and waved Isaac inside. Perhaps the girls at work were right. Perhaps he *did* have a woman somewhere. A woman with a child. So much for Paula's assertions that it couldn't hurt to try to breach Edward's reserve.

All the same, there was nothing wrong with taking a lift from him, and Charlotte couldn't deny that this was a great deal nicer than the bus. Not having to continually grab at her bags to get them out of the way of someone else's feet. Isaac safely strapped in behind her, with Stinky on his lap. Leather seats. The quiet strains of music floating at her from four different directions. She began to relax.

'It would be more convenient for you to drive to work.'

As they passed Regent's Park Edward's customary forthrightness broke the silence.

'Yeah. More expensive, too.' She grinned at him. 'Congestion charge, parking costs.'

He nodded. 'I thought you were going to say you liked the bus.'

'It's not so bad. You meet a lot of interesting people on buses.'

'So it's a social experiment, then?'

Maybe for Edward. It was a matter of necessity for Charlotte. 'You could call it that. We like it on the top deck, don't we, Isaac?'

'Yeah. You can see into people's windows,' Isaac piped up from the back seat.

'Can you?' Edward paused for thought. 'What do you see?'

'Christmas trees.'

'In July?'

'No, at Christmas.' Isaac's voice took on the tone of patient explanation that he sometimes used with adults. 'We counted how many Christmas trees we could see on the way home.'

'So you're a mathematician. Is that why you're called Isaac? After Isaac Newton?'

Isaac seemed to have succeeded where the combined talents of the Hunter Clinic had failed. That was definitely a joke, even if Isaac didn't appear to understand it.

'Who?'

Charlotte rolled her eyes. 'He's five, Edward.'

He nodded. 'So you're keeping Newton for later.' He made it sound like leaving the best chocolate in the box until last. He raised his voice, speaking to Isaac again. 'So how many Christmas trees did you count?'

'A million.'

'Really? You live on the moon?' Edward's lips twitched and Isaac cackled with laughter. Although neither seemed to be quite on the same intellectual wavelength, they clearly shared the same sense of humour.

'Noooo. Kentish Town.'

'That explains it, then. Are you sure you didn't count any of them twice?'

Isaac shrugged. 'Maybe. It might have been a hundred.'

It seemed so natural to laugh with them. The obvious thing to do. 'It was three hundred and forty-nine, wasn't it, Isaac?'

'That's right. Three hundred and forty-nine.'

Edward nodded. 'Impressive. That's a prime number, you know.'

'What's a prime number?'

Edward shot a helpless glance at Charlotte and

she shrugged. All of a sudden this quiet, reserved man had become almost talkative, and against her better judgement she actually wanted to hear what he had to say for himself.

'It's...um...it's a very special number. There are lots of them. I dare say they'll teach you about that at school.'

'When?'

'Er... Pretty soon, I imagine. Ask your teacher.'

'Okay.'

Lucky escape. Charlotte mouthed the words at him and he raised one eyebrow, as if he'd been in complete control all along.

'How many are there?'

She saw the line of Edward's jaw stiffen as it became apparent that she had spoken too soon.

'More than you can count. Even if you ride on the bus all day. The first prime number is two. Then five...'

By the time he'd worked his way up to twenty-nine and shown no signs of flagging Charlotte decided to step in. At this rate they could be driving to Birmingham and back before either Isaac went to sleep or Edward got to the point where he could no longer work out the next prime number in his head.

She turned in her seat to face Isaac. 'Edward's got to stop counting now, sweetie, because he's driving and has to keep his eye on the road. I'll explain all about prime numbers when we get home.'

'Okay.'

It was nice having her in the car. She smelled good—like soap and roses. Rose soap, maybe. Edward ran through all the possibilities in his head and surprised himself with how delicious each of them was.

She didn't just smell nice; she *was* nice. Whenever he saw her with the clinic's clients she was always the same. Gentle, reassuring, and yet with a hint of fun about her. She made people smile. But Edward couldn't help but think there was more. When he'd seen her at the bus stop the other day, huddled under her umbrella in the pouring rain, there had been a defeated slant to her shoulders that had made him want to stop, but his nerve had failed him. Getting involved with people wasn't what Edward did.

'You must like jazz?' She was stretching her legs out in front of her. Smiling.

'Very much,' he said. 'You?'

'I don't really know. I've not listened to much. I like this.'

'Good.' He could have left it at that. Would normally have left it at that. But against his better judgement he wanted to prolong the conversation. 'Most people just automatically say they love jazz, irrespective of whether they've listened to any.'

She gave a little laughing nod, as if she knew just what he meant. 'It's one of those things that you're meant to like, isn't it? I mean if you admit to not knowing much about jazz, then it's like owning up to being some kind of barbarian.'

'I don't think you're a barbarian.' He thought she was a damn sight more honest that most people.

He was rewarded with one of the smiles that she was so free with. This one seemed just for him. 'That's all right, then.'

Charlotte asked him to drop them in the High Street, but when Edward insisted on taking her all the way home she directed him to a quiet back-street. Small houses—many of them shabby and unkempt. He parked outside a house with a neat front garden. The front door badly needed a paint job. Charlotte jumped out of the car, unbuckling Isaac's seat belt while Edward took her shopping bags out of the boot.

'Can I carry these in for you?'

'No. No, that's okay, thank you. Thanks for the lift.' She picked the bags up with one hand and took Isaac's hand with the other. 'I'll see you on Monday.'

'Bye, Edward. Thank you…'

She shot a glance of approbation in her son's direction and then turned away. Suddenly it seemed that she couldn't get rid of him fast enough and a vague feeling of disappointment nudged at him.

'Bye, Isaac. Nice to meet you…'

The boy twisted his head around as his mother marched him away, and gave him a grin, but Charlotte seemed caught up with her shopping bags. There was nothing to keep him so Edward got back into his car. As he turned in the road he noticed in his rearview mirror that the front gate was sticking and that she was struggling with it. He almost stopped the car and got out again, but then she kicked it and it snapped open, and she walked up the front path without looking back.

Charlotte slammed the front door closed behind her and dropped her shopping, leaning back against the door. Home. Half of her wished she was still in Edward's car and that they really had been driving to Birmingham and back. Newcastle, even. The other half was glad that he was gone before he'd had a chance to see the threadbare carpet in the hall and the second-hand furniture in her sitting room.

'Is Edward your boss, Mum?'

'He's a surgeon. At the clinic.'

'So he makes people well? Like you do?'

'Yes, darling.'

Isaac nodded. 'He's nice'

Charlotte found herself smiling again. 'Yes, he is, isn't he?' She picked up her shopping bags. 'Now, let's see what we've got for supper, shall we?'

It was only a short drive from Edward's house back to Charlotte's, but it was like travelling from one world to another. The trendy shops and cafés gave way to houses which seemed even more run-down than they had yesterday evening, and when he drove slowly along Charlotte's road it didn't seem any more salubrious than the last time he'd been here.

Perhaps he shouldn't have come. At ten o'clock on a Saturday morning she could be out, or having a lie-in...anything. But he was here now, with

Stinky sitting next to him on the front passenger seat. If she wasn't there, then maybe Stinky would fit through the letterbox.

Cars lined the pavement, and he had to drive past her house to find a parking spot. As he did so he caught a glimpse of her on the doorstep, between the broad backs of two men who seemed to be crowding close in on her. What he could see of her stiff, upright frame, screamed that there was something wrong.

Edward accelerated into a free space. 'Don't move, Stinky. I'll be back in a minute.' He lunged out of the car, and down the road, to where her front gate stood open.

'Charlotte!' Now that he was closer he was sure that he was right. She was dressed in sweat pants and a tee shirt, bare feet on the doorstep, but she stood as tall as she could, the door almost closed behind her, her face fierce and determined. 'What's going on?'

She stared at him as if he'd just landed from another planet. One of the men swung round to face Edward, his pudgy face harsh. 'Nothing to concern you, sir. Just a bit of business with the lady.'

Her face had flushed bright red. Tears rimmed her eyes, before she quickly brushed them away.

These guys were bad news. They stank of the kind of aggression which dressed itself up in cheap suits and a nasty attitude.

'Then you have business with me.' Edward pushed in between them and stood next to her on the step. He wanted to put his arm around her, ask her if she was all right, but this wasn't the time. 'Step back. Now.'

They stepped back. The anger that was raging in his chest must have been showing in his face, because the expression on the face of the larger of the two became slightly less belligerent. Edward pressed his advantage. 'Now, what's all this about?'

'Are you this lady's husband, sir?'

'I'm her legal advisor.' Suddenly Edward was mightily glad that he'd left Stinky in the car. This was rapidly beginning to look like a confrontation of some sort, and holding a battered blue rabbit in his hand wouldn't have helped.

He felt Charlotte's fingers on his arm. 'No, Edward. Please.' Her voice was almost a whisper.

If she wanted him to go, she had another think coming. Edward didn't shift his gaze from the two men. 'Who are you? Do you have some identification?'

One of the men reached slowly into the inside pocket of his jacket and drew out a wallet. Opening it, he held it out for Edward to see.

Debt collectors. What had Charlotte got herself into? No time for that now. A child's whimper sounded from the other side of the door and he felt Charlotte's small, convulsive movement against his arm. 'Go inside, please, Charlotte. Close the door.'

She looked up at him. Cheeks pink, her lovely eyes still brimming with tears. She hesitated, obviously torn between going to comfort her son and dealing with the men on her doorstep.

'Go and make sure Isaac's okay.' He spoke gently to her and she nodded quickly, disappearing inside the house.

One down, two to go.

He turned to the two men. 'I assume you're not in possession of a court order with regards to this property?'

'No, sir.' Somehow the man made that sound like a threat.

'In that case I'm asking you to leave now. I'll speak to you when you're standing on the pavement.'

The men exchanged a look. Obviously they considered that browbeating him was a different mat-

ter from a lone woman and a child, and Edward
didn't bother to conceal his disgust as they turned
and took their time in walking down the path.

'There is the matter of an unpaid debt, ma'am.'

Edward looked round and saw Charlotte back
in the doorway, pulling a pair of sneakers on. She
must have settled Isaac and come back out again.

'You don't speak to her. If you've something to
say, then say it to me.' Edward had just appointed
himself, unasked, into the role of protector, but
he didn't care. No one else was around to do it.

'I need to speak to the lady.' The man's voice
suddenly became gentle. He'd seen a way in and
was trying for it. Be nice to her, then divide and
conquer.

Edward looked round at Charlotte. It was one
thing to expect her to go along with his instructions at the clinic, but here... Here she had Isaac
to think of, and she wasn't going to give that responsibility away too easily.

'You can speak to my...' She walked down the
path and stood next to him. 'My legal advisor.'

The man pressed his lips together. 'In that
case...' He turned to Edward. 'We're looking for
this lady's husband. We have reason to believe
he's here—'

'He isn't,' Charlotte broke in vehemently. 'I haven't seen him for over a year.'

'We'd like to check, madam.' Deftly the man had turned back on Charlotte.

'You have no right of entry to this property. The lady's already told you that the person you're looking for isn't here, and that she doesn't want you in her home.' Edward folded his arms to indicate that this was now an end to the matter.

'Fair enough. But do you know where he is?' The question was aimed at Charlotte again.

This time she gave her answer to Edward. 'I don't...'

He nodded, laying his hand on her arm with as much tenderness as he could muster. 'They're allowed to ask you whether you know where the person they're looking for is. It's entirely up to you whether you answer or not.'

'We haven't lived together for eighteen months. I have the name of his solicitor.' Her voice was almost a whisper, her eyes pleading. Not just for him to help her get rid of these men. For him to understand.

'Can we have that at least...please?' The word *please* seemed to stick in the man's throat and he took another step forward, as if this was an invitation into the house.

'Wait there.' Edward turned to Charlotte and she nodded. She knew as well as he did that if she could give these men something it might get them off her back. 'Go and get it, then.'

She hurried inside and Edward indulged in a staring contest with the men, open hostility buzzing between them. She returned, clutching a piece of paper with a hastily scribbled address on it, and gave it to Edward. 'Here it is.'

Edward turned back to the men on the pavement. 'Right. The lady hasn't seen her husband in months, and she doesn't know where he is. She's given you every assistance she can in locating him, and this ends her involvement in the matter.'

'All right.' The man snatched the paper that Edward proffered. 'And you're sure you don't know where he is?'

'Doesn't sound very likely to me,' his companion sneered, forcing home the point. 'Doesn't he want to see his own kid?'

Edward heard Charlotte's sudden intake of breath and fought to stay in control of the fury that swept over him in a red-and-black wave. Much as he'd like to, getting into a fight with these guys wasn't going to help. 'You've asked your question and you've got your answer. You know full well that the law prevents you from harassing this lady any further or from speaking to a minor.' He pulled his phone out of his pocket. 'You've got ten seconds to get going before I call the police.'

The two looked at each other, grins on their faces. Edward wondered how many people actually followed through with that threat. He started to thumb the numbers on the screen.

'All right, mate.' The larger of the two, who was obviously the lead man, held up his hands in surrender. 'We're going.'

'Tell your head office to expect a letter, confirming the information that this lady's given you. She knows nothing more which will assist you, and she wants no further contact with you.' Edward pressed his advantage home.

The two turned without a word and Edward watched them lumber off down the road and climb into a shiny SUV. Business was clearly booming for them.

'Go and see to Isaac. I'll just keep an eye out here for a couple of minutes.' The SUV roared past them down the road, with the engine being gunned so that it made as much noise as possible.

He looked around. Charlotte was still there, her face burning so red that he probably could have warmed his hands on it if he'd needed to.

'Thanks, Edward. I'm sorry you had to see that.'

'It's not your fault. Those guys had no right to act the way they did.'

Her gaze dropped to the cracked paving stones at their feet. 'Yeah, I know. It was such a shock to see them on the doorstep, and they were so intimidating...' She looked as if she was about to burst into tears and then visibly pulled herself together.

Turning, she hurried back up the path and opened the front door. 'I'm really grateful to you, Edward. I'll...' She had the grace to flush an even deeper red before she gave him his marching orders. 'I'm sorry, but I need to go and see how Isaac is. Will you excuse me? I'll see you on Monday.'

The door closed, and Edward found himself standing alone. What was he supposed to do now? Charlotte had made her intentions more than clear, and he supposed he should leave. But he was damned if he was going to leave a woman and child alone in this situation.

Edward strode to his car, snatched Stinky up from the front seat, and walked back to her front door.

CHAPTER THREE

ISAAC WAS WHIMPERING in her arms. He was trying to be brave, but his little body was shaking as he clung to Charlotte. She wanted to go and find those men and punch them. More than once.

There was a noise at the letterbox and she tried not to jump. Isaac fell silent, staring at the door.

'Charlotte? Charlotte, I have Stinky here. That's what I came for this morning. He's too big to put through the letterbox.'

She thought about telling Edward to leave him on the doorstep. She might possibly have been able to, whatever the consequences later on, if she hadn't seen the look on Isaac's face. It was as if he'd just seen the cavalry, riding hell for leather over the horizon.

Perhaps he was right. Maybe his five-year-old mind was able to see a little more clearly than hers. She wouldn't be all that surprised. Edward engendered such a plethora of different emotions in her that her judgement wasn't to be trusted where he was concerned.

'I'm coming...' she called out to him, and took Isaac's hand, leading him to the door. She took a deep breath and opened it.

She had hardly registered it before, through her tears and her panic, but Edward's eyes looked a brighter blue than usual. His hair darker. There was less of the suit and tie about him and a great deal more of the enigma, with his dark shirt and jacket giving him an almost dangerous look. Even the blue stuffed toy, grasped lightly in his long fingers, couldn't dispel the feeling that here was a hero, come somehow to save her.

'Hey, Isaac.'

He might only have been able to spare her son a half-smile, but it would have melted an ice hotel, launched a battleship, and cracked a grin on the face of a statue.

'I brought Stinky for you.'

Isaac looked up at him and wiped his nose on his sleeve. Charlotte resisted the impulse to tell him to use a tissue on the grounds that she'd been doing the same herself just a moment ago. This morning Isaac could do anything he liked, as long as she could see just a glimpse of his smile.

'Thank you.' Isaac's voice was small, quavering, and it tugged at Charlotte's heart.

'Bit of a morning, eh, little man?' Edward suddenly seemed to realise that getting down onto Isaac's level would be a good idea and dropped to one knee, proffering the boy's toy.

Isaac nodded, reaching for Stinky. Charlotte felt his hand slip out of hers and he walked uncertainly towards Edward, then seemed to throw all caution to the winds and flung his arms around Edward's neck.

'Hey... Hey, there.' For a moment Edward's hands fluttered awkwardly. Then he wrapped his arms around Isaac, hugging him as if he could hold him tightly enough to make everything all right.

For a moment all Charlotte wanted was to be in on that hug.

'You know what?' Edward had got to his feet, taking Isaac with him. Safe and sound in his arms. 'You and I have a job to do. We're going to tell your mum that everything's going to be okay. That we'll look after her.'

Isaac nodded sagely.

'I think we could all do with a cup of tea. What do you say?'

'I want milk.'

'Good idea. I'll have some milk, too. And we'll make your mum a cup of tea.'

'She likes coffee. The kind with the froth on top.'

Isaac had a tight hold of Edward's jacket collar, his other arm wrapped around Stinky. Charlotte knew that his tears weren't too far below the surface, but Edward seemed to be reassuring him with his sheer bulk and unflappability.

'Okay. Tell you what—we could go out for coffee, if you'd like.' His gaze moved from Isaac to Charlotte. 'What do you think?'

'I...' She wanted his arms around her so much. His comfort. Charlotte pulled herself upright, squaring her shoulders. 'We're all right. Really.'

'Yeah. I can see that.' He reached forward, touching her cheek so lightly that she shivered. As his hand dropped to his side his fingers skimmed his thumb, as if he wanted to test the exact nature and volume of the tears he'd brushed away.

'We can manage, Edward. I don't know what I would have done if you hadn't turned up just then, and I can't tell you how much I appreciate it...' Good start. That was really going to make him feel that it was okay for him to go away now, wasn't it?

'But…?'

'But I can't keep you. You must have things to do.'

Edward always had something to do. His head was always buried in a book, or some papers. Even when she'd chanced to see him in the street he was always deep in thought, and half the time he didn't even acknowledge her, either because he hadn't seen or didn't want to see.

'I don't think so. In fact I've nothing to do today. It's only fifteen minutes over to my place.' He pursed his lips, as if he'd surprised himself by the invitation as much as he'd just surprised Charlotte. 'We'll get coffee on the way, and we can talk… privately. Perhaps I can help.'

She could have turned his help down for herself, but she had Isaac to think about, and Charlotte had no choice but to grab at any and every offer that came her way. And there was the matter of that nagging need at the back of her head, which wanted her to explain to Edward, tell him that she wasn't the person that all of this made her seem. She was going to have to swallow her pride and go for coffee.

* * *

Edward had waited in the hallway while she dragged on a pair of jeans, shoved her feet into her sandals and splashed her face with water. Her eyes had looked puffy in the mirror, but she hadn't wanted to keep him waiting for too long, so she'd dropped her make-up bag into a canvas holdall along with a few of Isaac's favourite toys to keep him occupied.

They'd stopped at a coffee shop and Edward had ushered them in. Isaac had slipped his hand into Edward's, tugging at his jacket until he'd lifted him up to see over the counter. He seemed to trust that if he stuck with his new friend no harm would come to them, and Charlotte hoped that her son was right.

Now they turned into a wide street, dappled by sunlight shining through the branches of the trees. Turned again into a short drive, behind a high wall hung with greenery, and came to a halt outside a double-fronted Georgian house, white-painted with slim, elegant lines.

It was quiet here. Far enough from the main road for them to be able to hear birdsong. Charlotte handed Edward the cardboard coffee holder and busied herself with getting Isaac out of the car.

The silence between them was oppressive. Edward seemed awkward as he opened the front door, walking inside without even asking them in, and Charlotte began to wish that she was anywhere but here. Apart from being at home, that was, waiting for the phone to ring again.

'Well...' He clapped his hands together awkwardly, like a man who was unused to guests. 'Here we are.'

'Yes.' Charlotte stepped tentatively over the threshold, holding tightly onto Isaac's hand. Inside the house it was tranquil—a cream-painted hallway, pictures on the walls, green plants everywhere.

'Let's go into the sitting room.' Edward seemed to galvanise himself into action and opened a wide panelled door, ushering them through it.

Sunlight streamed through the front windows onto pale oatmeal-coloured sofas at the front. A TV, nestling unobtrusively in one corner, conceded pride of place to a state-of-the-art sound system. The room ran the full depth of the house, and next to the French windows at the back stood a grand piano.

'What a lovely room.' She gave her son's hand a squeeze, although whether it was to give or receive confidence she wasn't quite sure. 'Isn't it, Isaac?'

Isaac was too busy looking around to reply. At the lines of glass-fronted cabinets, heavy with books. The green plants, arching gracefully around the windows.

'Come and meet Archie.' Edward beckoned Isaac over towards the French windows, where a ginger cat lay stretched out on the carpet, basking in the warm sunlight.

'Is he a lion?' Isaac looked up at him gravely.

Edward laughed. 'Well, he's not very fierce. You won't need that.' He gestured towards Isaac's plastic ray gun, which he'd insisted on bringing along with him.

Isaac stowed the ray gun in his pocket, just in case he'd need it later, and followed Edward over to where the cat lay. He watched solemnly as Edward tickled its ears and then its tummy as it rolled over, luxuriating in his touch.

'Do you want to stroke him?'

Edward was letting Isaac approach the creature in his own time, and Charlotte smiled as Isaac slowly reached out.

'He's growling.' Isaac snatched his hand away.

'No, that's purring. It means he likes you.' Edward drew back a little, letting Isaac stroke Archie.

'Be gentle with him, sweetie. Remember that he's much smaller than you are.' Charlotte stayed at her post by the door, still not sure whether to accept the quiet welcome of this place.

'Would Isaac like to watch some TV? While we talk?'

'Oh. Yes, he might do. Thank you.' Charlotte took the remote that Edward proffered and found a channel that Isaac liked, turning the sound down to a quiet murmur.

Edward set a low coffee table in front of the screen, put Isaac's frothed milk onto it and opened a cupboard, drawing out the molecule modelling kit.

Charlotte grinned. 'You're going to let him play with your toys?'

'If I share, then maybe he'll let me have a go with his ray gun. Will he be all right here?'

'He'll be fine. Look, he's already made a new friend.' Charlotte nodded towards Isaac, who was talking confidingly to Archie, stroking him carefully.

'Good. Well, we can talk through here.'

There was a door at the far end of the room,

by the piano, and Edward disappeared through it, leaving Charlotte to get Isaac out of his jacket and settle him in front of the television.

She took one last look at Isaac, and then took a deep breath. Time to face Edward now. Now that keeping up appearances was no longer an option it was going to have to be the truth. She just hoped that he would understand.

He was sitting at a table in the large kitchen, studying the coffee in front of him as if there was some solution in there. She could tell him the answer to that. She'd tried it enough times herself. She mustered a smile, and sat down opposite him.

'So who's Archie named after? Archimedes?' She pulled her own coffee towards her and peeled off the plastic lid. It was smooth and strong and the caffeine hit her straight between the eyes.

He looked up, suddenly aware of her presence. 'Yes, actually. Although it's a mispronunciation, of course. Am I that predictable?'

'No. I thought of the most unlikely thing I could and suggested that—' She broke off as he smiled at her. That smile did all kinds of things to her, none of which were going to be of much help at the moment.

'So.' His gaze dropped to his cup again. 'You're in trouble, aren't you?'

'Yes. I am.' She should have realised that Edward would cut straight to the point. He wasn't much for small talk. Charlotte hadn't anticipated how much of a relief it would be. 'It isn't what you think.'

He looked up at her. Those deep blue eyes were almost irresistible. 'I'm not thinking anything.'

'You're always thinking something, aren't you?'

A trace of a grin tugged at his lips. 'Yes, I suppose I am.'

Suddenly she wanted to defend herself from all the implications of what Edward had seen and from whatever conclusions that agile, razor-sharp mind of his was working its way towards. 'The debts aren't mine, Edward.'

'I know. It was your husband they were looking for…'

'He'll be my ex-husband soon. Very soon, if everything goes as planned.'

Maybe she should have been a little less vehement about that. Said it a little more as if it was a matter of fact rather than an avowal of innocence. Edward seemed far more at home with facts than emotions.

'Have you asserted your separation financially?'

'Yes. There are no more joint accounts and credit cards. The house and the mortgage are in my name.'

'Then you have nothing to worry about. As long as you've applied for a Deed of Separation, and you're not jointly liable for any of his debts...'

'How do you know all this?' The question had occurred to Charlotte on her doorstep, but she'd pushed it to the back of her mind.

'I have a degree in Law.'

'As well as being a surgeon?'

'I...um...I was advised to wait until I was eighteen to go to medical school. I was at a loose end.'

'So...' The gossip was correct, then. 'You *are* a genius?'

'They called it "gifted" when I was a kid. Now it's called High Learning Potential.'

The twitch of his lips told Charlotte that they were just labels, which Edward didn't set much store by.

'I don't need to be a genius to know that there's more to your situation than what you've told me.'

There was a lot more. Charlotte grinned at him almost automatically, the way she did whenever anyone offered anything that sounded a bit too much like sympathy. 'Really?'

'Yeah, really. And you're not going to convince me otherwise with that smile, either. Even if it is a very nice one.'

Stop now. One thing at a time. Having Edward as a concerned friend was already turning her universe upside down. It was a bit too soon for compliments.

'You're right, that's not all. My husband had…I think it's probably fair to say *has*…a gambling addiction.'

'And that's why you left him?'

'I wasn't that smart. I didn't know about it until the bailiffs started calling. The first one was the day after Isaac's second birthday.' She sighed. She didn't need to go into details; he was getting the gist. 'I started out by paying his debts. He promised me that he'd stopped, and I believed him.'

'But he lied?' He was blunt, but there was no brutality there. Just the truth.

'Yes, he just kept on racking up the debts. Internet gaming sites, card games… He maxed out our credit cards and I dipped into the money I'd inherited from my parents just to keep a roof over our heads.' Charlotte gulped in a breath of air.

This time she was going to do things better. She had to for Isaac's sake.

'But you couldn't hold it together.' Another flat, emotionless statement of the inevitable facts.

'I did for a while. Then he left. That was eighteen months ago. I sold the house, paid off all the debts, and managed to scrape enough together for a deposit on a smaller house. Made a new start for Isaac and me.'

Edward just nodded.

Caught in the force of his concentration, Charlotte realised that Edward was not an absent-minded, other-worldly creature. He was thinking things through, his ruthless single-mindedness not allowing a single detail to escape.

'Does your husband know where you are?'

'Yes, he knows. I was hoping that he'd come and see Isaac but he never has.'

Charlotte heaved a sigh. She didn't need to tell him about the thing that had damned her the most—it didn't affect the problem at hand. Anyway, it was humiliating. Even more so than having to admit she was being chased by her husband's debtors.

She met those blue eyes again. Ever questioning, but not as judgemental as she'd feared.

'And you said your divorce is in the pipeline?'

'Yes. I have the Decree Nisi and I'm waiting for the Decree Absolute. I'm hoping that he won't throw any spanners into the works and put in a last-minute objection.'

'Do you have any reason to think he will?'

'No… Maybe… I don't know. Peter's not exactly the most predictable of people.' Charlotte sighed. 'He's not strong. He'll do whatever gets him through the day and forget all about the consequences for tomorrow.'

'You don't trust him.'

Damn right she didn't. She had very little reason to. 'No, I don't. The men who called this morning aren't the only people looking to get paid. I had a telephone call last night from someone who said I owed money for a mobile phone bill.'

'Do you?'

'No!' She was protesting too much again. 'My phone's a pay-as-you-go…'

Charlotte reached for her handbag to show him the phone and Edward stopped her, laying his hand on her wrist.

'It's okay.'

'It isn't. The divorce won't protect me if he's

managed to raise a line of credit in my name, and I've no money to pay off any more of his debts.'

It was as if she and Isaac were being dragged back into the nightmare that she'd worked so hard to get out of, and there was nothing she could do about it. Charlotte gulped back the tears, pulling her hand away from his grasp.

'What did you tell them?' He was still calm, almost icy cool. Still focussed on the facts.

Charlotte took a deep breath. She should try to sound a little more grateful, Edward had already helped her more than he had any reason to. 'I said that I had no knowledge of the account in question and asked them to put everything in writing and send it to me.'

'Good. We can start making enquiries on Monday. In the meantime, is there anyone that you and Isaac can stay with?'

'Not really. My parents are dead and I don't have any brothers or sisters…' She tried to smile, make light of it, but Charlotte had never felt so alone. 'We'll be okay. I'll take the phone off the hook and lock the door…'

'You'll stay here.' Even Edward seemed surprised at his uncompromising words.

'No! I mean…Edward, it's kind of you to offer, but I couldn't think of it.'

'What about Isaac? I gather that Sunday mornings are a favourite time for debt collectors to make their calls. He's old enough to know what's going on now.'

Low blow. He'd found the spot where her guilt was almost unbearable. 'I thought he was too young to remember. But when those men called this morning…'

Isaac had understood exactly who they were and had launched himself at them, trying to drive them away, trying to protect her. Charlotte had managed to keep hold of him, and the men had smirked at each other as she bundled him back into the house.

She heard Edward sigh.

'Look, you need to get yourself and Isaac out of the firing line for a few days, until you have a chance to sort this out. I've plenty of room here—there are two spare bedrooms upstairs—and you'll both be safe.'

He didn't mince his words, or dress it up to make it sound as if she had a choice, but he was right. She *did* need to get her son away from this nightmare, and she had nowhere to take him.

'Charlotte.'

He reached out to her, his finger tipping her chin upwards. His shrewd blue eyes saw straight through her. There were no excuses, no way that she could just fob him off with something.

'Where else are you going to go?'

CHAPTER FOUR

HE HADN'T MEANT to be cruel, just to look at the situation rationally. But when she finally gave way to her tears, her forehead sinking until it almost touched the surface of his kitchen table, her body trembling with the effort that it seemed to take her to cry, Edward realised that she wasn't the only one who was in over her head. He didn't feel equal to this—not the crying woman at his kitchen table, or the vulnerable child on his sofa—and the knowledge that he was way past the point of dispensing some good advice and leaving them to it wasn't helping much.

'Hey.' He reached out, touching her arm tentatively with the tips of his fingers. 'Charlotte, please don't.'

She ignored him, and it had been a stupid thing to say anyway. Charlotte was at perfect liberty to do whatever she wanted. It was him who didn't want her to cry, because it wrenched his heart so much to see it.

'Okay. Well, you can cry as much as you like. But I'd appreciate it if you'd keep it down a bit or Isaac will be in here, blasting me with his ray gun for upsetting you. Which I didn't mean to do, by the way.'

Her shoulders stopped shaking. Slowly she raised her head. For a moment Edward was unsure about whether she was going to burst into laughter or start crying again. He decided to wait. He'd probably said more than enough already.

'I'll pay you rent.' Her voice was low, a little unsteady, but there was no doubt that she was back in control of herself.

'No. I won't accept it.' She opened her mouth to protest and he silenced her with a look. 'That's not negotiable.'

'I could clean for you.'

'That's not going to work either. I have a cleaning lady and there will be hell to pay if you put her out of a job.'

Somehow, from somewhere, she managed to find a smile. It was like basking in a ray of sunshine on a rainy day. 'I wondered whether it was you who kept all these plants watered.'

'We have an...understanding. She looks after Archie and the plants, doesn't move anything that

I'm working on, and I keep out of her way and don't forget to pay her. Works like a dream.'

'I'm sure it does. Does she cook?'

'I imagine so. Not while she's here, though.'

'I'll cook for you, then.'

She narrowed her eyes obstinately and a sudden flood of longing gripped him. He hadn't counted on these sorts of complications, and wondered whether what he was about to do was wise.

'Okay. Deal.'

She bit her lip. 'Isaac won't be any trouble. He won't touch any of your things. I'll make sure of it...'

That sounded a bit dull. 'I can put anything that I don't want touched away out of his reach. And he can be as much trouble as he likes.'

She gave a tremulous laugh. Charlotte wasn't just a pretty face; she was tough, too. And brave. And about a million other things, all of which he felt inexplicably driven to find out more about.

'You have no idea how much trouble a determined five-year-old can be and, trust me, you don't want to find out.'

'Well...I'll leave that to you. What I mean is that you should make yourselves at home.' His mother was always telling him that this house was far too big for one. Granted this was not what she'd had in mind, but the principle was a good one. There was more than enough room for him to carry on with his life, undisturbed by two house guests.

'Thank you. I really appreciate this, Edward. And it'll only be for a few days, while I get everything sorted out.'

'You can stay as long as you like.'

He knew that it would take longer than a few days to work this out, and he didn't want her or Isaac going back home until it was. They'd both been through too much already.

After he'd taken them back to Charlotte's house, to pack what they needed, Edward had left them to their own devices. They had their own routine, which clearly involved eating and sleeping at regular intervals, and he had his, which disregarded any such practical activities in favour of whatever he happened to be doing at the time.

When he parked outside his house on Sunday evening his mind was still racing from the concepts that had been explored in the afternoon seminar he'd attended, and then endlessly again afterwards over sandwiches. The house was dark, and as he slipped his key into the lock on the front door it occurred to him that Charlotte might have taken her son and left, leaving a note on the hall table for him to find when he got back.

'Oh, no, you don't...' He muttered the words to himself, since she wasn't around to hear them.

He slid the key into the lock and the door gave by six inches, then caught. The chain, which usually hung unused from the frame, barred his entry. At least he wasn't going to have to get back into his car and drive over to Charlotte's house, to make sure that she and Isaac were all right.

All the same, there was the small matter of being locked out of his own home. Ringing the bell would probably wake Isaac up, as would bellowing through the letterbox, so Edward pulled the door to, twisting the key to relock it.

He seldom took the path around the side of the house, and he jumped as a pair of iridescent orbs appeared from the bushes. 'Locked out as well, eh?' Archie swished his tail. 'Yeah, I know. It's a bit much.'

Discomfiture that his arrival home hadn't provided the usual well-ordered release from the complications of the world began to swell into anger.

He didn't need to find the key for the French

windows; they were standing open. She was there, in the failing light, curled up in a chair on the stone-flagged patio.

'Charlotte!'

She jumped, throwing off the woollen jacket that was wrapped around her shoulders and twisting around. When she saw him she smiled, and Edward felt the hard edges of his anger melt.

'It's you...' She rubbed her eyes with her hand, as if she had been dozing.

It occurred to Edward to make the point that there wasn't much to gain by locking the front door if she was going to fall asleep with the doors to the patio wide open. But that sounded rather too much like criticism, and he'd already seen her flinch enough times when she or Isaac did something that she thought he might disapprove of.

'Did I wake you?'

'I must have just dropped off...' Her gaze swung from him to the house and then back again. 'Ohhh. I locked you out...'

That didn't seem so much of an issue as it had a moment ago. 'Putting the chain on the front door's a sensible precaution at night.'

'And falling asleep with the patio doors open isn't.' She gave a little self-deprecatory smile.

He shrugged, as if he'd not thought about that. 'Why don't you give yourself a break? You're safe here. No one can find you.' No one apart from him. He liked that thought so much that he dumped his briefcase on the stone flags and pulled up a chair, sitting down next to her.

She nodded. 'Thank you. Having a safe place to stay has meant a great deal to me and Isaac.'

'So you've had a good day?'

'Yes, thank you. We had lunch and then went to the park. They've got a great playground there, and a lovely cafeteria. We played football, as well.'

She made it sound like a real treat, and Edward found himself smiling, wondering whether football wouldn't have been preferable to a dark, humid lecture theatre. She and Isaac were a small, self-sufficient unit, though. They probably wouldn't have wanted him along.

'Sounds nice. Have you thought about what you're going to do yet? With regard to your situation?' He tried to put it delicately.

'I called Paula and she's going to lend me her laptop tomorrow. I've drawn up a list of things I need to find out about, and then I can start in on sorting everything out.'

Edward had left his own laptop on the coffee

table, specifically so she could use it if she wanted to go on the internet. He should have thought that she wouldn't touch it, or allow Isaac to either, without asking. 'No need for that. Mine's right there.'

'Oh. Thank you.' There was a hint of awkwardness in her manner as she slid to the edge of her seat. 'Would you like something to drink? There's some hot chocolate...'

Her determination to pay her own way seemed to know no bounds. Everything he did for her—things that he gave without expecting anything in return—was entered on a balance sheet in her head to be repaid at a later date. Edward was debating whether he should tell her that she really didn't need to wait on him like this, but she was on her feet already.

'Hot chocolate would be great. Thank you.'

Since she so much wanted to do something for him, he supposed he should let her, and Charlotte's bright smile as she disappeared into the house tentatively proved his theory.

She brought him a mug of creamy hot chocolate, along with a plate of home-made biscuits.

'Thank you.' He took a sip and nodded his approval. Archie materialised from his nightly tour of the garden and curled up under her chair. If she'd been feeding him as well as she seemed intent on feeding Edward he couldn't fault the animal's change of allegiance. 'There's something I want you to do for me.'

She brightened noticeably. 'Yes, of course. What is it?'

Too late, Edward realised that he should have chosen his words more carefully. The impression that she was about to do him a favour was accurate enough, in the context of the amount of thinking time he'd already given to her plight, but Charlotte probably wouldn't see it that way.

'My father has his own practice at law, and I want you to consider making an appointment to go and see him. He can advise you and get his investigative team to find out exactly what's going on. With my dad on your side, you can get things sorted out quicker and more efficiently.'

'But I can't afford to pay a lawyer, Edward.'

'You won't need to. If I ask him, he'll do it for free.'

She hesitated. For a moment Edward thought that her pride was going to let her see sense and give in to expediency. Then she shook her head.

'No, I can't do that. It wouldn't be fair. Please don't mention it to him.'

He sighed. 'What isn't fair is that you're spending time on researching and fighting your own battles when there are people who will happily help you out. It's not just you that it makes an impact on—it's your work at the clinic.'

That particular argument didn't stand up to much scrutiny. Charlotte must have been worried sick over the last couple of weeks, but she'd never shown any evidence of it on the job.

She frowned at him. 'I wouldn't let anything get in the way of my work.'

'I know you wouldn't mean to, but none of us can be expected to give a hundred per cent when we're under the kind of pressure that you're facing at the moment.' He was pressing hard, exploiting every chink in her armour.

She hesitated. 'Edward, I... You're confusing me.'

Well, now she knew how *he* felt. 'It's very simple, Charlotte. Trust me.'

Two little words, spoken almost as a throwaway to emphasise his point. He should have known better. If he'd thought about it for two seconds he would have realised that trust was something she had a lot of difficulty with.

'I'm sorry.' Without another word, she got to her feet and disappeared into the house.

Edward leaned back in his chair and stared out into the evening shadows. Archie slid past his legs, waiting to be stroked, and he ran his fingers thoughtfully along the cat's back. Adjusting to the complex myriad of emotions that Charlotte and Isaac had brought to the quiet peace of his home was proving more difficult than he'd imagined.

The green reflective eyes seemed for a moment to understand his frustration, and then Archie was off again, his instinctive urge to chase shadows getting the better of him. Edward silently wished him better luck than *he'd* had tonight.

Edward had left the house before she was up the following morning. Charlotte went through the routine of getting herself up and ready for work, and Isaac ready for school, almost on autopilot. She was well aware that she'd walked out on Edward in the middle of a conversation last night, and common courtesy demanded that if he decided to broach the subject again she should have some kind of reasoned answer for him.

'Mum…?'

'Yes, Isaac.'

'Is everything going to be all right?'

She sat down opposite him at the kitchen table. 'Of course it is. What makes you ask that, sweetie?'

Some kind of understanding of the situation they were in, perhaps?

Isaac shrugged. 'I don't know.'

His brow was still furrowed, perhaps as a result of the unerring radar that seemed to alert him whenever something was wrong, even though he didn't grasp quite what it was.

'Look, sweetie. Those men came to our house by mistake on Saturday—they weren't looking for us. We're staying here with Edward for a few days, while I get everything sorted out, but that's going to happen very soon. Everything's going to be okay.'

'Do you promise?'

He still lived in a world where she could make everything right. Those trusting eyes would give Charlotte the courage to face anything that the world could throw at her. They'd even give her the courage to ask just one more favour from Edward.

'Yes. I promise. Cross my heart.'

* * *

She'd gone straight to Edward's office when she'd arrived at work and left a note for him on his desk. As luck would have it, he returned from his morning's surgery just as Allie and Paula were both within range of the nurses' station, beckoning Charlotte into his office in full view of both of them.

She was aware that two pairs of eyes were following her every move, so knew she'd better make this quick. 'I wanted to apologise. For last night...'

'You have nothing to apologise for. Why don't you sit down?' He threw himself into his leather chair.

'Because...' Charlotte shifted uncomfortably from one foot to another. 'We said we'd be discreet about our current living arrangements. And we're being watched.'

'Really? By whom?' He glanced around his office, perfectly oblivious of the stares that were homing in on them through the glass.

'Don't look...'

His attention swung back to her, and Charlotte began to wonder whether it wouldn't have been better to leave well alone. Edward's gaze made her feel as if he were undressing her. Taking his time and getting it absolutely right.

'There—will that do?'

As long as he didn't keep it up too long. 'That's fine. Allie and Paula are at the nurses' station. Watching us.'

'Ah. Well, in that case, I'll just pretend to show you this…' He flipped through the pile of journals on his desk, pulling one out and opening it. 'Then you can sit down and pretend to read it.'

His lips twitched slightly as she took the journal from his hand, and Charlotte suppressed a grin. His sense of humour might be an acquired taste, but it was well worth the journey.

'You wrote this?' She read the title of the paper slowly, just about getting the gist of it.

'Yeah.' He leaned forward across his desk. 'What do you think?'

'I don't know. Give me a couple of months to work my way through it…'

'Then you'll need to sit down.'

Charlotte gave up the unequal struggle and plumped herself down on one of the deep-cushioned leather easy chairs which were reserved for guests. Edward swung around in his own office chair, making sure that his back was to the glass wall, and shot her a conspiratorial look.

'So what do you want to speak to me about?' His finger nudged at the note on his desk.

Charlotte took a deep breath. 'I was being pig-headed last night. I'm sorry.'

'You have nothing to be sorry for. I'm not...' His intent blue gaze found hers and held it fast. 'I'm not great with certain kinds of solutions.'

What did he mean by that? Edward's usual forthright way of expressing himself seemed to have deserted him for the moment. 'I don't understand what you're saying...'

He sighed. 'I'm saying that I'm not as good with people as you are. I can be insensitive at times.'

'No, Edward...' She wanted to take him by the shoulders and shake this nonsense out of him, but she was being watched. She had to stay still and pretend this was just a conversation between two work colleagues. 'You've shown me and Isaac nothing but kindness.'

His eyes betrayed his confusion. 'Is this your way of letting me off the hook?'

'No. I'm paying you the respect of being honest with you. The way you've done with me.'

His slow smile penetrated every dark corner of

her being. Filled her mind with the kind of ideas that she'd been trying not to think about for the past three days.

'Thank you,' he said.

'You're welcome.' Charlotte was sure that there was a more appropriate response than that, but she couldn't fathom what it might be at the moment. Not without the kind of body language that would get her into deep trouble. 'Look, what I wanted to say was that I'm over trying to make out that I can do everything by myself. If the offer's still open, I'd be really grateful if your father could spare a little of his time—perhaps just to talk to me and give me some general advice.'

He nodded. 'The offer's still open; there was no time limit on it. I'll give him a call.'

'Thanks, Edward. I really appreciate it. You'll tell him that, won't you?'

'I will.' He pointed to the journal in her lap. 'You know, if you're going to do this properly you should at least look as if you're reading.'

She picked up the journal and looked at it. 'Better?'

'Much. If anyone asks, what's our excuse for talking to each other?'

'I've probably been disputing some of the conclusions you came to in this article.' Charlotte jabbed her finger at the page in front of her and threw the journal down onto his desk.

'Very theatrical.' His eyes flashed as he leaned forward, picking up the journal and clipping something to the pages before he passed it back. 'Here's my father's card. I'll give him a call right now and tell him to expect your call this afternoon.'

'You're enjoying this, aren't you?'

'I wouldn't say *enjoying*. I think you've made the right decision....'

'I meant the secret rendezvous stuff.'

'Oh. Well, that adds a certain frisson. D'you think it's working?'

'Probably not. But at least I've got a measure of deniability.' Charlotte slipped the business card into her pocket and closed the journal, passing it back to him. 'Will you be working tonight?'

'No. Do you want a lift home?' He grinned. 'You could wait for me by the park gates if you like. With a wig and a pair of sunglasses, no one will think it's you...'

'I'll wear a pink carnation in my buttonhole.'

'Yeah. That would be a nice touch. Match your ears.'

* * *

Her ears weren't the only things which felt as if they were burning up when Charlotte walked back past the nurses' station.

'Not so fast.'

Paula's murmured words stopped her in her tracks.

'Sorry?' She was going to have to brazen it out.

'So what's the story, then? You and Edward North?'

'He was just showing me a paper he'd written. In one of the journals. Something that came up.'

Charlotte pushed her hands into her pockets and curled her fingers around the business card, just to check that it wasn't about to leap out of her pocket and embarrass her even further.

'Well, make sure that something comes up more often. After all…' Allie shrugged '…one thing might lead to another.'

'I don't have time for anything like that. Isaac's the only man in my life at the moment.' It would be as well if *she* remembered that, too.

'Spoilsport. Surely you get time for a night off once in a while?'

Paula's tone was edged with concern. She might tease, but underneath it all she had a good heart.

'Edward North…he needs someone like you. And he *is* gorgeous.'

'And headed this way…'

Charlotte had been deliberately not looking in the direction of Edward's office and it was Allie who raised the alarm. Edward was striding towards them, and Charlotte caught the quick exchanged glance between Paula and Allie as he passed behind her. A little too close.

'Charlotte.'

There was something intimate about the way he said her name. Or maybe it was just her imagination. Charlotte didn't dare to look in Paula's direction.

'Mrs Ashe is here a little early with April. If you're free, then I'll see them now.'

'Yes, of course.' Charlotte reached over for the notes and followed Edward into the plush, comfortable consulting room.

The seventeen-year-old took a nervous breath as Edward began the careful, precise work of taking the dressings from the side of her face. The previous week he had used skin flaps to revise the scars that a road accident had left, and today April was to see the result. His small nod, and a

fleeting glance in Charlotte's direction, revealed
that he was pleased with his work.

'Does it look horrible?' April was chewing her
lip.

'No. Mr North's got to take a careful look, but
so far everything's fine.'

The other nurses sometimes complained that it
was pretty much impossible to gauge Edward's
reactions to anything, but today he seemed more
transparent than usual.

She ventured a little more reassurance for April.
'It's a little raised at the moment, but that's normal. It'll settle over time.'

'Yes.' Edward was taking her lead. 'I'm very
pleased with the way it's healing.'

Charlotte laid her hand over April's, feeling the
tremor of her fingers. 'When you look at yourself in the mirror, remember that we're at the very
early stages of healing right now. Your procedure
went well, and everything's going just as it should.
You'll see a lot of improvement in the coming
months.'

'That's okay.' April managed a smile. 'I know.'

She might be young, but April was much more
pragmatic than some of the clinic's clients, who
seemed to expect that the miracles Edward per-

formed should take effect immediately. Charlotte reached for the mirror, but Edward already had it, and was handing it to April.

'Everything's looking good, April. There's very little swelling, and I can see you've been doing all the things that Charlotte told you to do when we saw you last. Keep up the good work.'

'Thanks.' April took the mirror and looked at her reflection. 'That's not so bad.'

Charlotte grinned at her. 'No. Not so bad at all. Now, I'll show you how to massage it gently. With just a little more work, we can make it even better.'

CHAPTER FIVE

The smell coming from the kitchen was gorgeous. Mouthwatering. Edward wondered how he could possibly be so hungry when normally he ate far later than this, and sometimes not at all if he got involved with what he was doing.

'Do you know what's for dinner, Isaac?' He sat down on the sofa next to the boy, who was fidgeting restlessly.

'Yes. Mum made it yesterday.'

'Would you like to share?'

Isaac thought for a minute, and Edward wondered if he ought to rephrase.

'Lasagne.'

'Sounds great. I like lasagne.'

'Me, too. I like it here, too.' Isaac thought for a moment. 'When are we going home?'

Edward glanced towards the open door of the kitchen. No Charlotte. She must be able to hear their conversation, but it didn't appear that she was going to help him out.

'Whenever you and your mum want to.'

'Can we stay until next weekend?'

'Yes, if you'd like to. What's happening next weekend?'

'The men are coming again.'

'No, Isaac…' Where was Charlotte when he needed her? She didn't seem to have any difficulty in turning up almost like magic whenever she was needed at a patient's bedside. 'Your mother's done nothing wrong. Those men aren't allowed to come back, and I'm going to make sure they don't.'

'How?' Isaac slipped off the sofa and approached Edward, laying both hands on one of his knees, clearly intent on a man-to-man talk.

Edward took a deep breath and leaned forward. 'That's a secret. But I promise you that we'll stop them from coming back.' He held out his right hand. 'You want to shake on it?'

Isaac gave him a puzzled look.

'Here.' Edward picked up his right hand and gave it a gentle shake. 'That means that I've made a promise to you and I can't break it.'

'Like that?' Isaac proffered his right hand and shook Edward's again.

'That's right. Just like that.' This was going better than he'd thought it might.

Isaac proffered his hand again. 'I promise I won't touch your piano any more.'

A noise from the kitchen door made Edward look up and he wondered how long Charlotte had been standing there.

'I'm sorry. He only played a couple of notes and I wiped the fingermarks off...'

'Don't worry about it.' He turned back to Isaac. 'How does not touching my piano unless you ask your mum or me first sound?'

'I won't touch your piano unless I ask Mum or you.' Isaac sealed the bargain with a handshake and then ran over to the piano stool. 'Can I touch it now?'

'No, Isaac, it's time for dinner. Go and wash your hands.'

Isaac pulled a face, but ran out of the room. Charlotte's eye was on him all the way.

'How do you do that?'

She'd picked up the lasagne, newly out of the oven, and was carrying it through into the dining room. Edward followed with the salad.

'Answer all the questions? I just tell him the truth.' She laid the dish down onto a padded table mat, her shoulders drooping suddenly, as if someone had loaded some extra weight onto them.

'Well, most of the time. I still want to shield him, but he's getting to an age when that's not so easy.'

Edward wondered whether he should mention the fact that Isaac plainly wanted to do the same— to shield his mother. Probably not. He shouldn't interfere.

She'd put a small glass vase of flowers on the over-large oval table, which Edward had never managed to fill but had bought because it balanced out the proportions of the room. He liked balance. Order and proportion helped him to think. Charlotte had laid a place for him at the head of the table, and he sat down.

It was the strangest feeling. Charlotte on one side of him, helping him to a generous portion from the dish and pushing the salad bowl towards him. Isaac on the other side, sitting on a cushion so that he could reach the table. It was almost as though they'd taken him in, rather than the other way round.

'Would you like some water?' Charlotte was still on her feet, leaning across the table to place a beaker of water in front of Isaac.

'No, thank you. Why don't you sit down? I'll get some wine.'

She hesitated. Clearly debating whether or not

she was going to allow him to contribute to the meal even in this way. 'Um...yes. Thank you. That would be nice.'

Edward got to his feet and went to the kitchen, fetching a couple of glasses and a bottle from the chiller. When he returned he was gratified to find that she'd done as he'd asked, and was sitting, her hands in her lap.

He placed a glass in front of her, uncorked the bottle and poured.

'Thanks. That's enough.'

She'd only let him half fill the glass but that was okay. It was the principle of it. Something had been accepted into the routine that they were building.

Isaac was watching his every move, eyes wide as saucers. 'Can I have some?'

'No, sweetie, this is for grown-ups.' Charlotte quietened him with a quick look.

'Pleeeease.' Isaac was obviously unused to not sharing everything with his mother.

'I've got something better for you.'

Edward gave him a conspiratorial grin and the boy quietened. He went to fetch a sturdier glass from the kitchen cupboard—not the fine crystal that he'd given to Charlotte, but a nice-looking faceted tumbler—and grabbed a bottle of sparkling raspberry cordial from the fridge.

'Here you are.' He set the glass in front of Isaac and filled it. 'Try this.'

He sat down, aware that Charlotte's smile was on him. It seemed to slide into his senses, warm and tingling, like fine brandy. Isaac took a sip from his glass and gave the same nod of approval that his mother had given when she'd tasted her wine. He was a part of this little treat.

Funnily enough, Edward felt a part of it, too. Eating together…praising Charlotte on the meal. Hearing the silly jokes passing between Isaac and Charlotte, which both of them expected him to laugh at, too. He was probably expected to tell a few, as well, but he couldn't think of any that they might like at the moment. But even that didn't seem to matter.

The doorbell rang.

Isaac jumped and would have spilled his drink if Edward hadn't put out a hand to steady it. Instead his fork slithered to the floor, bouncing across the rug and clattering noisily on the wooden parquet.

'Let's not answer that.' Edward shot a grin at the boy. Doorbells didn't appear to be his favourite thing at the moment, and who could blame him?

'It's okay.' Charlotte passed her own fork over to Isaac and bent to retrieve his. 'It might be something important.'

Isaac's gaze pleaded silently with him.

'So what if it is? We're eating.' A feeling of bravado, quite out of proportion with the deed, sparked in Edward's chest.

'But it could be a friend. Someone you know.'

Unlikely. And if it were they'd know him well enough not to give up after the first ring. Opening the door when the bell rang was one of those things that Edward classed as optional.

'If it is they'll ring again. Or phone me.' Edward generally picked up the phone. Unless he was in the middle of something really interesting.

She laughed. 'Aren't you even curious?'

Edward shrugged. 'It's probably someone wanting to sell me something.' And, anyway, he was making a point.

'And a man's home is his castle, eh?'

'Er...possibly. In a manner of speaking.' It was certainly somewhere that his mind could wander freely. Explore the nuances that everyday life seemed to ignore so heedlessly. He hadn't thought about the aspect of fortification, though...

Charlotte leaned towards him. 'It's just an expression. One size fits all.'

She was smiling at him, and that smile seemed to banish all thoughts of whether, either in truth or in paradigm, his home really was a castle. All he could do in the face of such unarguable persuasion was smile back.

'Yeah. Well, then, whatever size my home is...' he flipped a glance towards Isaac, hoping he'd get the point '...or I am, it's definitely a castle. Which means I don't have to answer the doorbell if I don't want to.'

Isaac seemed to understand and turned his attention back to his meal. Charlotte was more difficult to satisfy.

'So... Don't you think you're missing out on something?'

'Like what?' Like the world that she seemed to inhabit? The one where she seemed to navigate chance meetings and random conversations so easily.

'I don't know. That's the thing, isn't it?'

He shook his head. 'It's no one. And, anyway, we're eating.' He turned back to the plate in front of him. 'And this is very good.'

CHAPTER SIX

CHARLOTTE HAD STACKED the dishwasher, sat with
Isaac until he started to yawn, and then taken him
up to bed. She tucked him in, along with Stinky,
in the small second guest room which adjoined
her own, and closed the connecting door between
the two. Isaac had slept soundly for the last two
nights, and showed no signs of doing anything
else tonight.

Edward had seen to it that Isaac should feel at
home here. When he'd taken them both back to
the house on Saturday afternoon he'd filled the
boot of his car with Isaac's things—toys, games,
clothes—so that he shouldn't wake in the night
and find himself in a completely strange place.
Somehow the molecule modelling kit had found
its way up here, too, and Charlotte wondered
whether Edward had put it there. The thought
made her smile.

When she got back downstairs the room was silent. Edward was in an easy chair with his nose

in a book. Not wanting to disturb him, Charlotte retreated to the kitchen and set about cutting sandwiches for Isaac's lunch tomorrow.

It was awkward being alone with him. At work, and when Isaac was around, she had a reason to ignore the desire to touch him. Now it was just him and her, and the empty space between them seemed almost to be daring her to breach it.

She'd finished the sandwiches, and was sitting at the kitchen table wondering what to do next, when the door opened quietly.

'Hey.'

'Oh...' She jumped, almost spilling the cup of coffee in front of her. Suddenly she noticed that the deep blue open-necked shirt he'd pulled on when he got home emphasised the colour of his eyes. 'You're busy. I didn't mean to disturb you.'

He shook his head, as if the concept were new to him. It probably was. Short of a nuclear explosion, it was practically impossible to divert his attention away from what he was doing at work. 'You don't need to sit in here, you know.'

'Yes...I mean, no. I mean...I don't want to get in the way.'

'You aren't. I'd appreciate the company.'

He meant it. Edward who had always seemed

so aloof at work, so self-sufficient. And yet he'd surprised her by seeming to understand just how she and Isaac felt. There was a great deal more to Edward than met the eye.

'Me, too. I'll...make some coffee, shall I?' She looked at the mug of instant in front of her. 'Some fresh coffee.'

'That's okay. I'll do it.' His mouth quirked. 'Refreshments and snacks don't count as cooking.'

His quiet, dry humour curled around her like a delicious full-bodied chuckle. 'Oh. So you're beginning to chip away at our bargain, are you?'

'I don't think so. I don't remember any mention of brewing, looking in the fridge, or pouring.' He measured the coffee into the machine and switched it on. 'And I certainly don't recall having covered electrical appliances.'

She smiled at him. 'I'm going to have to watch myself, aren't I? Next time I make a bargain with you, I'll make sure I read the small print.'

Did that sound a bit too forward? Hopefully everything would be settled in a few days' time and she would be on her way back home. Edward would forget her as he moved on to his next project of interest.

'Yeah. Always read the small print.'

He flipped open the cupboard doors and pulled out two cups, his long fingers placing them precisely on the counter. He had a delicate touch. He had to have. Microsurgery was one of the most challenging disciplines in a challenging world. And Edward was the best at what he did—just like everyone else at 200 Harley Street.

He made the coffee and picked up her cup with his own, taking it into the sitting room, as if unsure whether she might follow otherwise. Charlotte perched herself on the sofa, casting around for something that she could make conversation about.

'This is a lovely room.'

He nodded. 'Thank you.'

'Do you play the piano much?' From the wide-ranging collection of CDs on his shelves, and the grand piano, Edward was obviously passionate about music. In the three days that she and Isaac had been here, though, he'd never once opened the piano. Never once switched on the high-end audio equipment.

'Most days. Do you play?'

'No. I love listening, though.'

He must have changed his routine because of

her presence. Maybe she could encourage him to change it back again.

Edward didn't move. 'I wouldn't want to wake Isaac.'

'You won't. He's upstairs and he's fast asleep.'

Maybe she shouldn't have asked. Maybe this was something private, that Edward didn't like to share.

It *was* something private—she could see it in the way he hesitated. But then he made his decision, jumping up and striding across the room. Charlotte tried not to notice the ease with which he lifted the heavy lid, or the way that his shoulder flexed as he propped it open. Suddenly his mastery over the large, shining instrument was physical, as well as just a matter of the mind.

Sitting down, he raised the lid from the keyboard and lowered his fingers onto the keys. 'Any requests?'

For a moment she couldn't think. Then Charlotte knew what she really wanted to hear. 'Something *you* like.'

He nodded. Charlotte was expecting something classical, but the soft strains of *Ain't Misbehavin'* started to float across the room. Mesmerised, she moved closer and he beckoned her over, shifting up on the long piano seat to make room for her.

She swallowed hard. The music invited her. The way he made the song sound as if it had been written just for her. His sensitive fingers stroked the keys. Charlotte wanted nothing more at that moment than to sit next to him, be a part of this world. *His* world.

He raised one eyebrow at her hesitation, and the music swelled in reproach. She gave in and slid onto the edge of the stool, angling her body away from his.

'You'll fall off...'

The music dropped to a few notes, played with his left hand, while his right arm curled around her waist, pulling her further onto the stool. She was not quite touching him, and the seat was plenty long enough for two, but that didn't seem to make any difference. She could practically feel his body moving against hers.

There were a few chords that seemed to be his own addition to the mix, and then he segued into *As Time Goes By.*

'Mmm. Love this one.' She closed her eyes and let the music wash over her.

'Yeah. Kind of sad... Haunting.' He added an extra verse and chorus onto the end and then smoothly moved on into another melody that she couldn't name, but which she recognised from an old film.

'You like this?'

'I feel I should be in a cocktail dress and expensive jewellery. Leaning against the piano and sipping…I wonder what they were drinking in *Casablanca*?'

He chuckled. 'Champagne?'

'You remember?'

'No. Just a guess. I've got a bottle somewhere, if you'd like some.'

Charlotte laughed. 'No. I don't have the cocktail dress.' Or the jewellery. Her mother's ruby necklace, the one that she thought she'd never part with, had been sold and the money spent on the bricks and mortar of her house. The one that she'd been driven out of just a few days ago.

He seemed about to say something, then stopped himself. Moved on to play another song. The soft, melancholy chords filled the air around them.

Suddenly the music stopped. 'Hey… Hey, what's the matter?'

She felt him turn, but didn't raise her head. She didn't want Edward to see the tears.

Too late.

His fingers touched her arm, hesitantly at first,

and then more resolute. She felt his arm around her and, try as she might, couldn't bring herself to break away from him.

'It's nothing. Just the music.'

'Much as I'd like to think that it was my playing that moved you to tears, I doubt it.'

She wanted to hold on to him. It felt so natural to do so. But she shouldn't. She'd always been a sucker for the quiet type, and the last one she'd got involved with had almost destroyed her life.

'I...I'm just afraid that I'm going to lose everything. And you've been so kind...'

'You're not going to lose anything.'

He hugged her tight and she gave in and buried her face against the protective arc of his chest.

'Did you ring my father this afternoon?'

'Yeah. I've arranged to leave work early tomorrow and go and see him.'

'Good. You can stop worrying, then. He'll sort this out for you.'

'I know. Thank you. I'm just being silly.'

She felt his fingers stroking her hair. Just for a moment, before he snatched his hand away again. This must be torture for someone like Edward. So self-contained, so controlled. He didn't really *do* tears. She tried to move away from him, but his arm kept her firmly in place.

'You're not being silly. You lost everything once. It's natural to fear that it'll happen again.' He drew back, holding her shoulders tightly. Bending to capture her gaze in his. 'It's not going to. You're going to fight it.'

'I haven't got anything to fight with. All my savings are gone, and...' She couldn't even say it. The money was just a number. It was the loss of little things that she'd hoped she'd always keep that hurt the most. Memories...presents that people had given her over the years. The cot which, at one time, she'd hoped might see some more use. All Isaac's baby stuff. It hadn't fetched much, but every penny had counted when she'd been trying to put the deposit on the house together.

He shook his head. 'I wish you'd told someone. The clinic might have arranged an employee loan, or if not...' He pressed his lips together, apparently not wanting to finish the 'or if not'.

'I'd only been there for a couple of months. I was just glad to have the job. The extra income meant I could make the mortgage. Anyway...it would just have been another debt that I couldn't pay back.'

'So you sold everything you had?' His grip on her shoulders relaxed and his hands slid down to her elbows.

'Pretty much.' Charlotte put it to the back of her mind. 'But that's okay. Things are easier now. I've had a pay rise, and the first year's always the worst with a mortgage.'

'And I guess the extra shifts come in handy?'

He'd noticed, then. The way that she grabbed every bit of overtime that came her way, even though it meant that she had less time to spend with Isaac. 'Yes, they do.'

'You've worked hard. No one's going to take that from you. Just explain everything to my father and let him sort it out. And in the meantime you can stay here. Isaac seems...well, he doesn't seem to mind the arrangement.'

'You've made us both very welcome. Being here has been so good for Isaac.' It was Edward who had been good for Isaac, not the house. Providing a broad pair of shoulders that her son felt he could rely on. For that matter, he'd been good for Charlotte, as well.

'You can stay as long as you like.'

'Thank you. But we won't outstay our welcome.'

Like always, his smile was reticent, hard won, but all the better for it.

'Then I think we'll be okay. I can outlast you.'

No doubt he could. At the moment Charlotte reckoned that she had about ten minutes before she made a fool of herself and threw herself into his arms if she didn't find something to distract him.

'Will you play something else?'

Edward couldn't get the image out of his head. Charlotte in a dark figure-hugging dress. Something sparkly at her wrist and around her neck and a glass of champagne in her hand. Leaning against the piano, the gold flecks in her eyes reflecting the light better than any jewel could.

He played for a while on autopilot, while he added the fine detail to his vision. Then the real Charlotte broke in, her body warm and moving to the rhythm next to his.

'You'll have plenty of offers if you ever decide to give up the day job.'

Her smile made him stop thinking and start feeling as he ran his hands across the keyboard in a short, improvised cascade of notes.

'I used to play in a bar. When I was at medical school.'

'Yeah?'

'It paid better than stacking shelves. And I got to keep the tips as well.'

'Tips are always good.'

'Yeah. Made a big difference.'

'I bet you spent them on books.'

'Um... Yeah. Okay, you're making me feel predictable again.'

With Charlotte he could begin to fathom what people saw in small talk. It was easy. Delightful. Maybe they were getting a little too close to flirting, but that would be okay as long as he kept playing. Somehow the music made pretty much anything permissible.

She laughed. 'I think you're one of the most unpredictable people I've ever met.'

'Dancing to the beat of a different drum, you mean?' People had said that to him, and *about* him, all his life. That he was gifted. Different. That he didn't need the company of his peers as much as he needed to fulfil his potential.

'*Is* it a different drum? I rather thought that it was the same drum, but you just hear it a little more clearly.'

Edward let the thought percolate. 'That might be one of the nicest things anyone's ever said to me.'

The unexpected idea that words might not be enough to express his feelings on the matter occurred to him. He wanted to hold her again.

She smiled and his theory morphed into a tried and tested fact. Charlotte's smile held so much more meaning than words, and he allowed himself to bathe in it, feeling its warmth lap against his skin.

He didn't know how long he played for, and didn't much care. However long she sat here next to him, her body melting into the rhythm of the music, it wouldn't be enough.

When finally she drew away, another of those gorgeous smiles on her lips, the world felt suddenly cold.

'You play wonderfully.'

He nodded in acknowledgement. 'You listen wonderfully.' It was more as if she'd been a part of the music, shaping the emotion and cadence with him, although her fingers had never touched the keys.

She laughed, getting to her feet. 'I should go and get some sleep, though. Thank you for a lovely evening.'

'My pleasure. We should do this again.' The words escaped his heart before his head could issue the caution against asking for trouble.

She flushed a little and nodded quickly. 'Goodnight, Edward.'

He played a short, quiet goodnight, listening to the sound of her footsteps on the stairs. Then he closed the lid over the keys.

Charlotte was everything that he held himself aloof from. The instinct and emotion that he saved only for his music seemed to bleed into her whole life. It was captivating—tantalising, even—but it was a language that he didn't know how to speak. However much she tried not to disrupt his life, however well-behaved Isaac was, the two of them had the power to turn his well-ordered existence upside down.

Archie roused himself, stretched, and joined him on a restless errand to the kitchen, which had no particular purpose other than his need to go somewhere. Edward poured himself a glass of wine from the bottle they'd opened at dinner, leaving Archie to pounce on his food bowl as if he hadn't eaten in years, and wandered back into the sitting room. The book that he'd abandoned in favour of going to talk to Charlotte still lay on the sofa, and he picked it up, flipping it open. This, at least, he knew how to handle.

CHAPTER SEVEN

CHARLOTTE KNEW THAT Edward would be here somewhere. She hated that she needed to see him so badly, but she had nowhere else to go. She slipped through the reception area, avoiding the last stragglers on their way out of the clinic at 200 Harley Street, and ran up the stairs.

Edward's office door was closed and locked, but she could see his jacket, slung over the back of his chair. There was only one other place that he could be.

She left her coat and bag on one of the chairs in the closed-up nurses' station and took the stairs down to the basement. The gym was in darkness, but she could see lights shining through the glass doors which led to the pool.

Suddenly her courage failed her. She'd already accepted too much from Edward. Already allowed herself to get too involved with his life. He was quiet and kind, creative and a little quirky. But then her husband had been quiet and kind, too.

She'd thought that she could see hidden depths in him, where actually there had just been an angry void that he'd sought to fill with the thrill he got from risking everything on the cards.

Charlotte turned. She knew that Edward was here, and that at this time in the evening he was probably alone. Walking away was the best thing to do. The only thing to do.

She'd go upstairs to fetch her coat. Then come back down again, using the back stairs, so that no one would see her.

'What are you doing here?'

She'd been so lost in her own emotions she hadn't even seen that there was anyone on the stairs below her. Instinctively she turned to run upstairs, but it was too late. Edward had seen her.

It *had* been him in the swimming pool. His dark hair was still wet, slicked back from his face, and his white shirt was open at the neck. Not sure what to say or do, Charlotte focussed on the logo splashed across the gym bag that was slung over his shoulder.

'Charlotte…?' He was standing two steps below her now, and they were face to face. 'What's the matter?'

'Nothing.' *Everything.* 'I just forgot something and popped back...'

The whole difficulty of dealing with Edward was that excuses were practically impossible to get away with—unless, of course, you had the time to construct a well-thought-out, fully featured alibi.

He raised one eyebrow in disbelief and shooed her up the stairs.

'Come to my office.' His keys were in his hand already, and he strode past the deserted nurses' station and unlocked the door, motioning her in. He slung his bag on the floor, in the corner, and sat down in his high-backed leather chair.

'I feel as if I'm being hauled up in front of the beak.' Small talk was the one thing that she was better at than Edward. Her only chance.

His brow clouded, but then he refused to take the bait. 'Why don't you sit down, then?'

'Do I need to?'

'You don't need to do anything. It's an invitation.'

He leaned back in his chair, propping one foot on the desk, and Charlotte slumped down into one of the visitors' chairs.

'So…what is it, then?' One last try at putting the ball in his court. Making Edward talk first.

'I…um…'

He seemed suddenly hesitant. Maybe she was going to get her way after all. They could go home, she'd make dinner, and then on the excuse of an early night she could go and cry into her pillow. That was the thing she should have done in the first place—not come running to Edward every time something went wrong.

He tried again. 'There seems to be something wrong. I was wondering how the meeting with my father went…' He backtracked slightly. 'Not in detail. I wouldn't presume to interfere with a confidential exchange between lawyer and client…'

There was no such thing as a simple question in Edward's vocabulary; there was always some accompanying detail. The way his mind worked made Charlotte smile, however bad things were. 'No. I'm sure you wouldn't.'

'It's just a broad brush enquiry. About whether you're happy as a result of…whatever it was that was said.'

'Your father was very kind.'

Straight spikes of hair had begun to fall across

his forehead, and when he smiled it looked almost rakish.

'Good. And apart from being kind...?'

'He's offered to represent me, and I've accepted. I gave him some details on the phone yesterday, and he's already got an investigator to follow up on them. He's thought of everything.'

Edward nodded. 'I imagine he has. There's no need to worry.'

Her heart was almost tearing itself apart with panic. 'No. I'm sure there isn't.'

He got to his feet, unhooking his jacket from the back of his chair. 'I guess I should call your bluff and just take you home, then.'

'Peter applied for a loan in Isaac's name. One of those quickie ones you can get on the internet.' Charlotte couldn't help it. She'd blurted out what she'd come to say—what she knew that Edward couldn't mend, but somehow wanted him to know.

He slumped back down into his chair, shock on his face. 'Did he get it?'

'No, thank goodness. And your father's going to do all he can to protect Isaac from that happening again.' Charlotte could feel her shoulders beginning to droop, but the effort of keeping her

spine straight was finally too much to do anything about it.

'And what about the phone bill that you were
being chased for?'

'He's putting pressure on the phone company
to leave me alone. It seems that there's a bit of a
mix-up with names and I might be facing a few
more where that one came from.'

His eyes narrowed. 'A mix-up? How could that
have involved *you*?'

She'd faced a pair of blue eyes and a sharp legal
mind once already this afternoon. Edward's were
as kind as his father's, but somehow much more
challenging. The truth had been easier the first
time around.

'When Peter and I were living together...'

Tears again. What must Edward think of her?

'Hey...' He rounded his desk, dragged one of the
heavy armchairs over towards hers and sat down
opposite her, leaning forward until his hands almost touched hers. 'It's okay, Charlotte. I just want
to help.'

All she wanted right now was to feel his arms
around her. If Edward was on her side she could
do anything, be all kinds of strong. She met those

blue eyes again. They gave her courage for the thing that damned her the most.

'The phone bill dates back to when Peter and I were living together. He must have taken the contract out in my name and...' She shrugged. 'I didn't know about that phone—it was his second one. He had someone else.'

His face became cold, as if she'd just slapped him. 'You mean he's expecting you to pay for the calls he made to his mistress? While you were living with him?' Edward shook his head angrily. 'Oh, no...you're not doing that.'

She reached for him, but he wasn't there. He was too angry now even to see her, and he sprang to his feet and started to pace the office like a caged tiger.

'Edward. Please, don't...Peter probably didn't think of it like that. He doesn't think anything through. The phone was registered at my old address and it's up to me to prove it isn't mine...'

'Don't make excuses for him, Charlotte.'

Her own anger flared in response to his. 'I'm not. I'm just trying to work out what happened...'

'And if you keep on taking his side you'll always be a victim.'

'Oh, so *that's* what you think, is it?' She was on

her feet, catching his arm, forcing him to face her. 'I am *not* a victim. I've stood on my own two feet since Peter left me, provided for Isaac...' She took a deep breath. Shouting wasn't going to do any good, and if there was anyone still in the building they'd be sure to hear them.

'I know.' Edward's rage turned abruptly cold. 'But this is not your responsibility.'

'No, it isn't. But there's another child, too—a little girl. She's not my responsibility either, but I still can't help thinking that somewhere out there that child's mother is going to be facing the same thing that I did. I might not like her very much, but I can feel for her.'

'There's a baby?'

'Not a baby—a child. She'll be three years old now.'

He didn't need to be a genius to be able to do that particular calculation. Peter hadn't just had someone else while he was living with her, he'd had a child as well.

'You've told my father this?'

'Yes. I said that he could do whatever it took as far as Peter was concerned, but that I wouldn't go out of my way to implicate his partner if there's been any fraud. That's my decision, Edward, whether you like it or not.'

Warmth bloomed in his face. 'Most people wouldn't be so forgiving.'

'I'm not either. I don't forgive her, but I won't hurt her daughter. She's no more responsible for any of this than Isaac is.'

'Maybe the best thing you can do for this woman is to show her exactly what she's got herself into...'

'That's what your father said.'

'Must be right, then.' A ghost of a grin shimmered on his mouth.

'I suppose so. But all I really want to do is to be free of Peter. Your father's agreed to review my divorce papers, to see if there's anything I've missed, and to do all he can to push it through without any hitches. That's a big weight off my mind.'

He nodded. 'My dad's not going to let you down. Once he gets his teeth into something he's like a dog with a bone, and he won't let up until he's got everything sorted out.'

She could smile now. His impassioned rage had shown that Edward didn't just pity her. He hadn't shrunk from demanding answers from her, asking the really hard questions.

'That's something you both have in common. I appreciate it more than I can say.'

He gave the customary small nod, which said he'd heard. A smile which said he'd understood.

'I should go now. I need to pick Isaac up soon.'

He shook his head. 'One more minute.' His back was against the door and he was leaning on it, his arms folded. 'I'm afraid it's no more Mr Nice Guy, Charlotte.'

She swallowed. Edward was getting darker and more dangerous again. She had to admit that she rather liked it.

'Really?' She took a step forward, tilting her head up to meet his gaze. If he wanted another confrontation he could have it.

'Yeah. You can put up a fight if you like, but you and Isaac are staying on with me until this is all sorted out. However long it takes.'

'We've had this conversation before…'

'And we can have it again if you want. You'll tell me that you don't want to impose, I'll say that you and Isaac are no trouble and that I like having you both around, and then you'll give me that look...' He grinned. 'The one that you're giving me right now...'

'And...?'

'And you'll say that you and Isaac have managed on your own up till now, that you don't need anyone.'

'That's not quite true...'

'No, it's not. You'll say it anyway, though, just to put me in my place.'

That smile of his didn't have a place. Neither did Edward.

'You're reading my mind now, are you?' Just as long as he couldn't access the part of her imagination that was engaged in stripping his shirt from his shoulders. Running its hungry fingers over his skin and allowing him to back her against the desk...

He narrowed his eyes and she shivered. There was something tender about the curve of his lips, something raw about the look in his eyes. 'I should warn you that I have a Joker up my sleeve.'

She nodded. 'Isaac. You'll say he's happy where he is and it would be wrong to put him through any more upset. That I might be able to see the debt collectors off, but I can't protect him from the stress.'

John North had said as much, advising her that if she had somewhere else to stay she should do so.

Edward nodded. His gaze flipped quickly to the sofa, which was relegated to the one corner of his office that wasn't lined with bookshelves, and then back again to her face. Maybe he really was reading her mind. The sofa would be admittedly more comfortable than the desk.

'And I'd be right?'

'Yes. You'd be right.'

The smile that made his eyes seem impossibly blue, the one that he had no trouble in sharing with Isaac, was all for her this time. 'Are we done, then?'

Not by any stretch of the imagination. 'I suppose so.'

'And your answer...?'

'Thank you. Isaac and I would like to stay.'

At least he had the grace to nod, as if the outcome of this particular skirmish hadn't been a foregone conclusion.

He stepped away from the door, hooking up his jacket and slinging his sports bag over his shoulder. 'Let's get out of here. What's for dinner?'

* * *

She'd tried to palm him off with peppered steak, but Edward had rather liked the idea of eating early and sharing pizza with Charlotte and Isaac. He liked the execution even better.

Isaac stood on a chair, a folded-down apron tied around him, dipping into bowls of sliced tomatoes and mushrooms to decorate his pizza. This was the kind of fun he hadn't had in a long time, and the feeling that the woman and child he so wanted to protect were here, safe with him...

Edward paused for a moment to consider whether *safe* and *with him* weren't in fact a contradiction of terms and then gave up the unequal struggle. For tonight it was more than enough to know that they were having fun, and that he was there to turn back anyone who came knocking on the door.

'So who's this meant to be, then?'

A grave face stared out at him from Isaac's pizza.

'It's...' Isaac had a showman's mastery of the expectant pause '...*you!*'

'Me?' Edward ignored the stifled giggle behind him. 'I don't look very happy.'

'That's your thinking face.'

'Ah. Well, I suppose that's all right, then.'

'What's yours?' Isaac peered across at Edward's pizza, and would have toppled off the chair if Edward hadn't shot a hand out to steady him.

'It's...just a pattern.' He was beginning to learn that details could get him into trouble.

Isaac twisted his head from one side to the other. Edward wondered whether the complex symmetry was really so beyond him, and came to the conclusion that somewhere, on a chiefly instinctive level, he understood.

'It's different from Mum's.'

Charlotte had decorated her pizza with swirls and curlicues of tomato, mushrooms and olives.

'Well, your mum and I are different. We like different things.'

'Hmm...'

Isaac returned to his pizza, adding another mushroom to Edward's brow to indicate a stray lock of hair, leaving Edward to contemplate the essential differences between himself and Charlotte and thank his lucky stars that Isaac hadn't asked him to enumerate them.

The evening was warm, and while the pizzas baked in the oven Edward opened the French doors onto the patio, spreading a cloth on the table and unstacking the chairs. They ate together in the evening sunshine, and as the shadows lengthened Isaac was allowed to get down from the table. Edward fetched a ball for him to play football in the garden.

'Mind the flowers, sweetie.'

Charlotte was down on her knees, her arms around her son, talking quietly to him the way she did when she had anything serious to say.

'You can play there, on the lawn, but don't kick the ball too hard.'

It didn't matter. Isaac could have flattened every last one of the flowers in his garden and Edward wouldn't have cared. But Charlotte was his mother, and she wanted to teach him respect for the things around him, so Edward said nothing.

'How are you doing?' As the daylight failed the light in her eyes seemed to fail as well. The effort of getting through today was beginning to tell on her.

She smiled at him. 'I'm fine, thank you.' Her gaze shot back towards Isaac as the ball veered close to the flowerbeds and he ran to pick it up. 'You've been such a star, Edward.'

Warmth suffused the whole of his body. Edward made a difference every day. The complex surgery he performed had the power to change people's lives, and it would be false modesty to claim that he didn't do it well. He wouldn't do it if he didn't believe that he excelled at it. But that was different. Somehow making just the slightest difference in Charlotte's life had the power to move him more than the considerable satisfaction he got from his job.

'I might see if Isaac wants a hand with the football in a moment.'

Her laugh was sweet and clear. Closer to the laugh that had filtered into his consciousness more than once at work, jolting him suddenly out of whatever he was doing.

'If he thinks he's got someone to play football with he won't give you a moment's peace. I don't want to keep you from anything else…'

The books would still be there tomorrow. So would the paper he was writing. This moment would be gone.

Edward stood, rolled up his shirtsleeves and prepared to take on the simple intricacies of the Beautiful Game.

She had put Isaac to bed and only returned downstairs for long enough to bid him goodnight. Edward knew why, and he hated it. She'd faced the day, but now she needed to fall apart—and she was determined to do that alone.

He spent a miserable hour trying to review the notes of a young surgeon he was mentoring, and then climbed the stairs. He could hear a quiet, muffled sound coming from Charlotte's room. She was crying.

Should he tap on her door?

No. Late in the evening, her bedroom, offering solace… Things didn't get much more hazardous than that. He'd have to comfort her, take her into his arms, perhaps. Feel the softness of her body against his own taut, screaming frame. It wasn't a good idea. On the other hand just carrying on along the hallway and going to bed was impossible.

Edward sank to the floor at the top of the stairs. Waited. If he couldn't console her, the least he could do was watch over her—even if she'd never know he'd been there.

CHAPTER EIGHT

CHARLOTTE GREETED HIM the next morning with hot coffee, toast and a smile. Her capacity to smile never ceased to impress Edward, as did her ability to bounce back from whatever life threw at her.

'So it's the Lighthouse this morning.' She seemed to be looking forward to it.

'Yes. Sure you're up to it?'

She'd already had a hell of a week, and it was only Wednesday.

'Of course.' She settled into the front seat of his car. 'Why? Do you have any concerns?'

'No. I think it's a great idea for you to come and talk to Mercy before she's transferred over into the clinic's care. I wish I'd thought of it myself.'

He had, actually. He just hadn't been quite sure how to broach the subject. When Leo Hunter had suggested it, Edward's concerns that he might be seen to be favouring Charlotte above any of the other nurses had been put to rest.

'Lizzie didn't tell me much about Mercy. Just

that she was very frightened about being in the hospital, and it took the nurses there a long time to calm her.'

'Yes, it did. That's why you'll be with her for all the procedures that we're going to do at the clinic. So that she's always got a familiar face to reassure her.'

She smiled. Mercy was going to love that smile. 'I'll do my best for her.'

Charlotte snapped into work mode as soon as they entered the doors of the hospital, following quietly behind him, listening carefully to everything that was said. Edward stopped at the nurses' station and caught the attention of a trainee nurse who seemed to have nothing to do.

'Will you get me Mercy's notes, please?'

The nurse jumped to attention, handing him the file. 'She had a good night last night. Woke up a few times, but she wasn't crying the way she did before.'

'Good. This is Charlotte King. She's going to be looking after Mercy when she comes to the Hunter Clinic.' He squinted at the nurse's name badge, because he couldn't for the life of him remember her name. 'Charlotte, this is Kendra.'

Charlotte ignored Kendra's dismissive look and

stepped forward. 'Hi, Kendra. It's good to hear that Mercy's been so well looked after here.'

Kendra sniffed, obviously feeling that her role as a very junior nurse at one of the best children's hospitals in the country made her in some way superior to Charlotte. She had a lot to learn.

'You're a qualified nurse?'

'Yes, I'm an RN. Working towards being a Nurse Practitioner,' Charlotte replied quietly. She didn't seem to mind Kendra's attitude, however much it rankled with Edward.

'Charlotte!' A voice behind them made her turn. 'How good to see you—how are you?'

The senior nurse who greeted Charlotte obviously knew her well. Kendra realised her mistake and disappeared out of range as quickly as she could, followed by a small smirk of satisfaction from Edward.

'So how's Isaac?' Sandra Morton gave Edward a brief nod and then turned back to Charlotte.

'Oh, growing up. He's going to school now.'

'Really? Yes, I suppose he must be. He was such a cute baby. And how's Peter?'

A small pause.

Edward wasn't sure whether he should intervene or not, and decided that Charlotte was perfectly capable of handling the situation herself. Much better than he could, probably. He started to leaf through Mercy's notes.

'Actually, I haven't seen him for a while. He left.'

'No! But he was such a nice guy—' Sandra stopped herself. 'Obviously not.'

'It just didn't work out. But everything's good now.'

'Great. I hear you're working at the Hunter Clinic?'

'That's right. I'm here with Mr North to see one of your patients.'

'Ah, Mercy. Well, I'm glad to see that you'll be looking after her. The kid's had a bad time, and she deserves the best.'

Charlotte grinned. 'She'll get it. Just as she has here.'

Sandra nodded. There was clearly a great deal of mutual esteem between the two women and it warmed Edward to see Charlotte being treated with the respect she deserved.

'Well, I'd better get going. Call me some time— or I'll call you. Maybe we can go out one evening?'

'Yes. It's good to see you, Sandra.'

Charlotte turned back to Edward, and he flipped a page in the notes in front of him.

'You can stop pretending to read now...' She leaned towards him, whispering.

'What makes you say that?'

'Your eyes aren't moving.'

Fair enough. Edward hadn't thought that anyone would notice that he was staring at the same word on the page in front of him, listening to what the women were saying.

'I know what it says, anyway.' He snapped the notes shut.

'Can you fill me in on Mercy's history? Before we go to see her?'

'Yes, sure.' Edward looked at the sign above the door of the conference room and saw that it was empty. 'Let's go in here.'

He sat down, and Charlotte took a seat opposite him. He'd seen her at the clinic, and he knew that she was great at her job, but she always made it seem so natural. This change in context let him see just how professional she was.

'We don't know much about Mercy's background. She's thirteen years old, an orphan, and was clearly fending for herself for a while before being picked up by one of the charities working in the area. They've found a new adoptive family for her, back in Africa, and by all accounts she's very happy with them. She's been going to school and doing well.'

'Sounds good so far. Have they accompanied her to the UK?'

'No, she's staying with a foster family. I've spoken with the mother and she seems to be doing an excellent job. The problem is that Mercy doesn't want to talk about what happened to her before she was taken in by the charity.'

'So you've not been able to take a detailed medical history?'

'Yes and no. We know what's the matter with her, but I'd like to know what caused some of her problems as well. For instance, she has a perforated eardrum.'

'Hmm... Not usually a result of trauma. Although it sounds like a good probability in this case.'

Charlotte pressed her lips together in thought, and Edward ignored the little thrill of pleasure that seemed to accompany all his dealings with her.

'Your first objective is just to let her get to know you, though. See if you can reassure her so that she feels she's got a friend at the Hunter Clinic. Any information you can get is a bonus.'

'Okay. What else do I need to know?'

'She's here for surgery on a healed Buruli Ulcer.'

'That's a bacterial infection, isn't it?'

Edward nodded, pleased that Charlotte wasn't slow in asking for more information when she needed it. 'Yes, that's right. A Buruli Ulcer is relatively easy to treat when it's caught early, but if it's not—as was the case here—patients can develop large ulcers which result in disabilities and restricted joint movement as the scars heal. In Mercy's case there was a contracture which had multiple joint involvements—hand, wrist and elbow.'

He scrunched his own arm up to demonstrate the way that Mercy's arm and hand had been folded tightly in on themselves and Charlotte winced.

'Poor kid. It must have hurt like nothing I can imagine.'

'She's been through a lot. But the operation to straighten the limb, grafting in new material where necessary, was a success.'

'You did it?'

'Yes.'

That warmth again, as if her smile were caressing him. Pride because she cared that it had been Edward who had carried out the precise skin and muscle grafts which would restore some of the movement in Mercy's arm and hand.

'How much mobility will she recover?'

He shook his head. 'Difficult to say at this stage. But the prognosis is good, and if she keeps her physiotherapy up she should do well. That's another thing I want you to look at. She needs to be committed to this, and to understand how important it is for her to continue the things that she's being taught when she goes home.'

'Right. Okay, then. So I'm working on her heart, not her medical condition.'

'Primarily. Although she's going to need nurse-led care at the Hunter Clinic and you'll be providing that.'

If anyone could do it, Charlotte could.

When Edward ushered Charlotte into Mercy's room she wasn't quite sure what to expect. She found that Edward hadn't been quite honest with her.

The girl's face lit up when Edward smiled at her. 'Hello, Mercy. How are you today?'

'I am well, Dr Edward.'

'I'm pleased to hear that. I've brought someone to see you.'

Mercy's dark eyes never left Edward's face. If he reckoned that his quiet kindness hadn't got through to her, then he was fooling himself. Charlotte began to wonder what she was doing here. Edward had clearly underestimated his own capacity to reassure the girl.

There was tenderness in his eyes as he spoke again. 'Nurse Charlotte is going to look after you when you come to see me at the clinic. She's come to meet you.'

Mercy gave Charlotte a small nod.

'I'll…um…leave you, then.' Edward seemed suddenly at a loss as to what to do next.

'No. Please stay. Just for a few minutes.'

Charlotte didn't share Edward's conviction that she could gain Mercy's confidence instantly, through some magical process that he knew nothing about.

She pulled up a chair and sat down next to Mercy's bed. 'It's nice to meet you, Mercy. I hope that I can be your friend.'

Mercy nodded again, clearly deciding to adopt a

wait-and-see policy. Charlotte was going to have to prove herself, but that was okay.

'I've brought you some pictures of my family.' She had photographs in her bag—of herself with Isaac when he was a baby, together with some more recent ones, and some precious images of her parents. 'Would you like to see them?'

'Yes.'

That was a start. Charlotte began with the picture of Isaac. 'This is my son. His name is Isaac, and he was born on a Saturday.'

Mercy studied the picture carefully. 'Then in my country he would be called Kwame.'

Edward's curiosity got the better of him and he leaned forward. 'For Saturday?'

'Yes.'

'I was born on a Friday.'

Mercy smiled. 'Nurse Efie.'

Charlotte grinned. 'That's a lovely name. Thank you for telling me. What's yours?'

'Abena. My English name is Mercy.'

'You have a lovely smile, Mercy Abena.'

Charlotte had been alone with Mercy for almost an hour when Edward's phone beeped. He checked the text which had just arrived and made for Mercy's room. Charlotte was waiting for him outside the door.

'Thanks for coming so quickly.' She looked nervous, moving her weight slightly from one foot to the other.

'You said "asap".'

Charlotte wasn't one of those people who peppered all of her communications with either 'asap' or 'urgent'. When she said it, she meant it.

'I've noticed something…about Mercy.' She seemed almost reticent to tell him.

'Right. What have you seen?'

'It may be nothing…'

'What have you seen, Charlotte?'

She took a breath and seemed to loosen up slightly. 'We were talking together, getting on fine, and then all of a sudden she seemed to zone out. It only lasted for a little over ten seconds.'

He nodded, turning the various possibilities over in his mind. 'The nurses have said that she seems very withdrawn sometimes. Do you think it could just be her mental state?'

'Maybe.' She clasped her hands together—a small, nervous gesture. 'It doesn't feel like that to me.'

'Okay. What *does* it feel like?' This wasn't his

normal method of diagnosis, but he was willing to give Charlotte the space to prove him wrong.

'I think she may be having Absence Seizures.'

'Epilepsy?'

Charlotte nodded. 'Her eyes rolled back, very briefly, and her eyelids fluttered a little. I leant forward and put my hand on her arm and she didn't react. Afterwards she didn't seem to have any recollection of what had happened.'

'That was quick thinking. Well done.' Most people would have attributed a short period of absence to being the daydream of a teenager, far from home and trying to block out what was happening around her.

'I could be wrong. I looked on her notes and no one else has reported anything like this.'

Edward shrugged. 'Which just means you're a bit more observant than the rest of us.'

It wasn't only that. Charlotte had a habit of looking at people when she talked to them, giving them her full attention. Until he'd met her he hadn't realised just how few people really did that.

She flushed pink with pleasure. 'So you'll take a look at her? Ask her about it?'

'Nope.' He turned towards Mercy's door, twisting the handle. 'You're going to do that. I'll watch and learn.'

She was cheerful and relaxed with Mercy, as if nothing had happened, sitting down by her bed and motioning Edward to do the same. Charlotte worked her way round to the subject of the seizure quickly, but deftly, as if it was just another routine set of questions which had to be asked.

'When we were talking together just now you seemed to lose me for a moment. Dr Edward and I would like to ask you about that, if it's all right with you?'

'There is...nothing.' The sudden look of hostility in Mercy's eyes spoke far louder than her words.

'I'm sure there isn't. But can we ask, all the same?'

Charlotte leaned towards Mercy, a look of gentle encouragement on her face, and Mercy shrugged.

'Okay, then. Well, you seemed not to hear or see me for a little while. Has that happened to you before?'

Mercy's gaze flipped sullenly from Charlotte to Edward, then back again.

'It doesn't make you a bad person, Mercy. A

little boy in my son's class at school has the same thing.'

'He does?'

'Mmm-hmm. The doctors can stop it, though. Dr Edward could stop it.'

'Can you?' Mercy's gaze fixed on Edward.

'Yes.' He wondered whether he should say more and decided not to. Charlotte would fill in any of the details that she thought were necessary.

'We'll have to do some tests.'

Apparently a quick wrinkle of the nose was enough to help describe a blood test to rule anything else out, and an EEG which would pick up any unusual electrical activity in Mercy's brain.

'They're okay. They don't hurt.'

'And you can cure it?'

'Of course. If it's what we think it might be, then it might well just stop all of its own accord when you get a bit older. In the meantime we can stop it.' Charlotte reached forward, taking Mercy's hand. 'But Dr Edward needs to know all about this first, so he can do the right thing.'

Mercy hesitated. 'Some people say that this is a bad spirit...'

'No. It's nothing like that, Mercy. Trust me. Sometimes we just...skip a beat for a few moments.' Mercy looked unconvinced, and Charlotte tried again. 'Dr Edward told you that he could make your arm better, didn't he?'

'Yes.'

'And he did, right?' She waited for Mercy's nod. 'Then ask *him* if this has anything to do with bad spirits.'

Mercy seemed disinclined to ask a second time, but Edward answered anyway. 'It's nothing to do with anything like that, I promise you. It's an illness, and we can make you well with medicine.'

Mercy nodded. 'I do skip a beat sometimes.'

'How often? How many times every day?' Edward leaned forward.

'Three or four. Sometimes more.'

Charlotte nodded, as if that was just the right number of times to 'skip a beat' every day. 'And how long has this been happening?'

Mercy shrugged. 'Always.'

'Mmm…' Charlotte seemed to approve of that, too, although Edward couldn't see its significance. 'So is it all right if we do the tests, then? Like I said, they won't hurt.'

'Yes, Nurse Efie.'

A quick nod of her head and she turned to Edward. 'Blood test?'

'It's what I'd do.' He couldn't resist teasing her, just a little. 'Want me to go and fetch a kit for you?'

She rolled her eyes at him to conceal her smile. 'No. I'll go.'

'Nurse Efie, eh?' Edward leaned against the railings of the hospital's roof garden, the breeze rearranging his hair into the maverick version of his usual clean-cut style. 'So come on, then. What's mine?'

'I didn't ask. You can find out for yourself. Mercy will tell you.' Charlotte took a sip of her coffee. 'She really likes you. Says that you're kind.'

'Does she?' The idea seemed to surprise him.

'So what's wrong with being kind?' She grinned up at him.

'Nothing. I try to be kind. I'm not as good with people as you are, though.'

'I think you underestimate yourself. Didn't you see her face when you walked into her room this morning?'

Either Edward didn't have an answer to that, or he wasn't sharing. 'So what made you cotton on to the name thing?'

'The mother of one of my patients told me, years ago. Apparently it's quite important which day you were born on in some parts of Africa. I just gave her the information about when Isaac was born to see if she'd pick up on it.'

Edward nodded. 'I'll have to find out a bit more about that...'

'Poor old Archie. He's not going to have his name changed, is he?'

'I don't think so. It would probably confuse him. Cats are all instinct and not much brain.' He took another sip of coffee. 'So I've put a call in to the Head of Neurology. Is there anything else I should know? I'm wondering whether there's any connection between the seizures that Mercy's been having and the burst eardrum?'

'I don't think so. We mainly just talked, but Mercy said that after her parents died she lived with an uncle. I think that was when she was beaten, because she said that her aunt made her deaf.'

Edward shook his head, staring at his coffee. 'Someone would have had to hit her pretty hard.'

'Yes. But she was having the seizures before then. So hopefully the two things are unconnected and the seizures aren't a result of brain damage.'

She looked up at Edward and he blinked quickly. Took a swig of his coffee, and then wiped his eye.

'Something in your eye?'

'No. Yes, probably.' Whatever it was it seemed to be a source of embarrassment.

'Want me to take a look?'

'I think I'll manage.' He took another mouthful of coffee. 'These kids... We have to do something...'

Charlotte laid her hand on his arm. Tried not to think about the way the hard muscle flexed at her touch and to convince herself that this was simple reassurance. 'You *are* doing something. You've given her back the use of her arm. She knows that, and she says that she's going to exercise every day.'

'It's not enough.'

'It's what we can do.'

If the other nurses at the clinic could see them now. Edward, impassioned and almost weeping over a patient. Charlotte, resorting to reason and logic. It was so unexpected as to be almost bizarre.

'I know.' He drained his cup and dropped it into hers, scrunching the two together to make a ball, which he lobbed into the nearest recycling bin. 'I want you there when Mercy has the EEG, to re-assure her that no bad spirits are out to get her. I'll clear it with Leo.'

'Thanks. And thanks for listening.'

'You were right. You've done a really good job here today.'

His praise meant a lot. More than a lot. Everyone at the clinic knew that Edward's praise had to be earned. Charlotte felt her cheeks flush with pleasure. 'Thanks. I'd like to just pop in and say goodbye to her before we go. Tell her that I'll be back soon.'

He grinned. 'Do that. Then I'd better be getting you back to the clinic, or Lizzie will have my hide for kidnapping you.'

CHAPTER NINE

IT WAS CLEAR when Leo Hunter telephoned to check whether Edward had anything he'd like to raise at this afternoon's review meeting that he was not expecting him to attend. Leo knew him well enough to understand that Edward's pledge to support the new charity arm of the Hunter Clinic was on the level of research, operating procedures and maintaining clinical excellence. It didn't involve attending meetings which didn't deal with those goals.

The usual procedure was that Leo informed him that a meeting was taking place, more as a gesture of courtesy than anything else, and Edward tendered his apologies and read the minutes when they were circulated. That had always worked perfectly.

'You mean you're considering some research?' Leo's voice sounded perplexed.

'No, not really. Well, maybe if something presents itself. I'm just interested in how we can help these kids outside of simply giving them the medical treatment they need.'

There was a pause and Edward shook the handset of his phone, wondering if the line had suddenly gone dead, before realising that Leo was just taking his time in getting his head around the proposition. Edward's forte had always been in the operating theatre, making clinical decisions and implementing them. That was his skillset. He usually left community issues to someone else.

'I'll see you later, then.' Leo still sounded a bit suspicious. *'We've had to move the time from four o'clock to six, in order to fit in with the operating schedules.'*

Edward's heart sank. Six o'clock. He'd been to his share of these meetings, and they were renowned for going on until late into the night. Usually he'd be the last to object, but tonight... Actually, he wasn't doing anything tonight. But he'd been rather looking forward to doing nothing with Charlotte and Isaac.

All the same, he'd just asked for this and it seemed grudging to turn it down now. 'I'm free at six. I'll see you then.'

Edward got home at ten o' clock. Isaac was already in bed, and he hadn't expected to have a meal waiting for him, but within moments of him depositing the armful of papers that he'd brought home onto the hall table Charlotte was calling him into the kitchen

'Is that enough?' She surveyed the full plate, with three different kinds of salad and a large slice of home-made quiche.

'Are you mad? You obviously don't have any idea what I usually manage to feed myself when I get home late.'

His diet was relatively balanced, and usually healthy, but when Edward was busy cooking didn't figure much in the equation.

She dismissed his customary eating habits with a small sniff and walked over to the fridge. 'Would you like some juice? Or there's some of that sparkling fruit cordial left over.'

'I'll have a glass of wine, if you'll join me.' Edward put his knife and fork down and got to his feet.

'Stay there. I'll get it.' She walked to the wine cooler and opened the glass door, her hand hovering over the rows of bottles.

'That one...' Edward indicated a light, fruity white, and nodded when she pulled it out, holding it up so he could see the label.

He was beginning to see what his father saw in

marriage. Not the meal on the table, or the fact that the lights were on in the house, but just that there was someone *there*. Someone to share the little things with—eating and drinking. Someone to talk to. Somehow the fact that Isaac was asleep upstairs and Charlotte was relaxing here downstairs gave Edward an immense feeling of well-being.

'I've got some treacle tart for afters.' She took a dish out of the fridge and put it into the oven to warm, then carried the bottle over to the table.

'Mmm. I love treacle tart. I haven't had it in years. And this quiche is really good, thank you.'

Edward opened the wine, and poured a glass for her. She took a sip and smiled.

'This is nice.'

The bottle probably cost more than the whole of the rest of the meal, but Edward wasn't about to tell her that. You couldn't buy what made the food so special and the wine so incidental. It was all about the cooking and the care that had gone into the preparation. About the knife and fork set precisely on the table, with a napkin and a glass. The flowers from the garden—just a couple of blooms—in a jug that usually lived under the sink.

'I've been stuck in a meeting for hours. It's good to get home.'

She raised one eyebrow. 'Which meeting was that?'

'Oh, one of Leo's. Reviewing the progress of the charity arm of the clinic.' Edward wondered whether she'd pick up on the unlikeliness of the whole thing.

'Really?'

If she had, it looked as if she'd decided not to ask.

'Yes. Leo seemed really pleased. There's a lot of progress being made.'

She nodded. 'So Leo and Ethan are getting on a little better?' It was an open secret that while the brothers remained professional in their dealings with the staff, they had what was euphemistically termed 'issues' with each other.

'Looks like it. Leo was praising Ethan's work, and Ethan looked genuinely pleased. A little bit surprised, as well.'

'I imagine Ethan felt he had to prove himself when he came back.' Charlotte was staring speculatively at her wine glass.

'I don't see why. Ethan's a superb surgeon.'

'Oh, Edward!' She narrowed her eyes at him.

'It's not all about how good you are at something. Ethan could be the best surgeon in the world, but he's still recovering from his injuries. He had to feel that there was an element of pity involved when Leo brought him back into the practice.'

'Yeah, I suppose anyone would. I think Ethan's realised that was never the case, though, and that Leo wanted him back for his medical skills. He was talking about the work that Leo had put into regaining the Hunter Clinic's reputation as well.'

'Really? That's good. Sounds as if they've got a bit more respect for each other now. So how's everything else going?'

'There are a lot of possibilities for expanding the charity side of the operation. Community issues to be taken into consideration—' He broke off as Charlotte hid a smile behind her hand. 'What?'

'*You've* been engaging in chit-chat about community issues, have you?'

He didn't blame her for her amused disbelief— he'd been both disbelieving and slightly amused himself. 'Well, someone's got to think about it.'

'And that's you, all of a sudden?' She couldn't disguise the warmth in her eyes.

'Maybe. We'll see. Anyway, I have some really

interesting opportunities in the pipeline, both at the clinic and at the Lighthouse Hospital. And there's an opportunity for me to join one of the teams visiting Africa for a few weeks. I'd like to hear what you think.'

He paused, aware that he didn't usually do this either. Edward made his own decisions about the way his career was going to go, without any reference to anyone else. But suddenly he not only wanted to tell Charlotte, he wanted to hear what she had to say.

'That sounds fantastic. I want to hear everything.'

She pointed at the food in front of him, which had all but completely slipped his mind in his enthusiasm.

'Finish your meal first, though...'

'Yeah. Then I'll tell you all about it.'

They talked for an hour, and then Charlotte's rapt attention was overtaken by fatigue. Edward turned to a book, and when he lifted his eyes after only a page she was asleep. He lifted her feet gently up onto the sofa, put a cushion beneath her head, and went back to his reading.

Calmed by the low sound of her breathing, he

let the words on the page fly through his mind, forming pictures and patterns as they went. It was as if her very presence made him more receptive—somehow more creative. The raw excitement of new thoughts, new challenges, reared up and dragged him headlong into the heady world of new possibilities that he so loved.

A sound penetrated his consciousness. Something outside in the hallway. The kind of thing that he would normally never heed, but which now somehow managed to jar all his instincts and set his nerves onto red alert.

He rose quietly and went to investigate.

'Hey, buddy. What's the matter?'

Isaac was at the front door, clutching Stinky with one hand and trying to pull the door open with the other. He ignored Edward, redoubling his efforts.

He should probably go and wake Charlotte. But she was sleeping so soundly, so peacefully. He could at least give this a go before he did so. Walking over to Isaac, he went down on one knee beside him.

'You want to go out?'

Isaac shook his head, giving the door one last tug.

'Ah, I see. You're just checking that we're locked up safely for the night. That no one can get in.'

Isaac nodded, staring at the floor as if he was being hauled up in front of the headmaster in disgrace.

'Right, then. That's a good idea. Let's do it together.' Edward imagined that Isaac probably wanted Charlotte to accompany him, and when the boy curled his arms around his neck he almost jumped back in surprise.

'Okay.'

'Well, let's fetch your dressing gown, then, so you don't get cold. And we can have a story afterwards if you'd like.'

Isaac nodded, and Edward hoisted him up in his arms. Lifting that small weight made him feel stronger than normal. As if he was some kind of superhero who could make things right and conquer all manner of monsters—even the ones in Isaac's head.

Surgeon and Dragon-Slayer General. Edward quite liked the sound of that. And if one involved precision instruments, the other involved a large sword which could be brandished flamboyantly when the opportunity arose. There was even a fair maiden, who was currently fast asleep on the sofa,

and an apprentice who was also asleep, worn out
by a brief but thorough inspection of the locks on
all the doors and windows and the first few pages
of his favourite bedtime story.

The last half-hour hadn't involved scaling any
high walls, or actually rescuing anyone, but that
was okay. Another time, perhaps, when the fair
maiden wasn't in such immediate need of her
beauty sleep.

Isaac stirred against him, snuggling up tight.

'Let's get you back to bed, little man.' Edward
whispered the words so as not to disturb the sleeping child, and rose, carrying the boy up to his bed.

And then, before he had the chance to think
about any such thing with Charlotte, he gently
shook her awake, turning back to his book as
soon as she had bidden him a sleepy goodnight.

CHAPTER TEN

IT HAD BEEN one hell of a tough week. The meeting with Edward's father, when the past had reached out, snatching her back into the nightmare that she thought she'd survived. Being afraid all the time, and trying not to show it to anyone.

One glass of wine with Edward on Friday, after Isaac had gone to bed, and she had fallen asleep on the sofa, waking with a start when she felt his hand on her shoulder, gently shaking her.

Today she woke to silence. A slow, sleepy climb into wakefulness, cocooned in comfortable forgetfulness. Something was missing, and she groped around in her mind for what it might be. No alarm. No… She sat up straight, propelled by panic. No Isaac, bouncing on her bed, telling her to wake up and get on with the day.

Hitting the floor at a run, Charlotte sped into his bedroom. The curtains were drawn back, the room was bathed in sunshine, and the bed was neatly made. Then she heard a noise from downstairs: Isaac's laughter, threaded through with Edward's quiet, rich chuckle.

Stupid. There was nothing wrong, no need to be this jumpy. All the same, she crept downstairs, just to check on them.

They were so involved with what they were doing that they didn't see her. Isaac was sitting on the edge of the sofa, next to Edward, with the coffee table pulled up in front of him so he could reach the keyboard of Edward's laptop. Edward, leaning back on the sofa, was concentrating hard on the screen.

'Way to go, partner!' Edward's face lit up and Isaac threw his arms up above his head, bouncing up and down on the cushions. Edward leaned forward, hitting a key. 'Do you want to try the next one?'

'That's all my teacher told me to do…' Isaac turned to him.

'Well, we don't need to do exactly what she says.' Edward shot him a look that mirrored the mischief on Isaac's face. 'You don't have to stop unless you want to. You're pretty good at this.'

'Okay…' Isaac giggled '…partner.'

Edward chuckled and pressed another key. It looked as if the two of them were fine without her for a while, and Charlotte could take her time in the shower.

When she got back downstairs, showered, dressed and feeling better than she had for weeks after a good night's sleep, she smelled coffee. The patio doors were open, and Isaac's voice drifted in from the garden.

'Is that a fresh pot of coffee I smell...?' She followed the aroma into the kitchen and found Edward there.

'Yep. Want some toast?'

'You are a wonderful man.'

He looked over his shoulder, shooting her a rakish half-smile. 'If I'd known that it just took a pot of coffee and some toast...'

'And a good night's sleep. Where's my alarm clock?'

He nodded at the clock, sitting innocently on the kitchen table. 'I happened to wake up early. I heard Isaac rambling around, and I sent him into your room to get it. I reckoned you could do with a bit of a lie-in.'

'Oh, so you've been enlisting my son in your machinations, have you?'

'Yep. He seemed to think it was a good idea, too. And I reckoned that if you did wake up, then you'd probably be a little happier to find Isaac creeping into your room.'

A good deal more relaxed, maybe. Happier...? That would depend on what Edward was there for. Charlotte dismissed the thought, and with it her fantasies of waking up to find Edward there.

'Has he had breakfast?'

'Yep. I told him that I'd be in trouble with you if we didn't keep to the straight and narrow, and he took me through the procedure step by step. Cleaned his teeth, had a wash, showed me where his clean clothes were. Do you *always* let him have chocolate biscuits for breakfast?'

'No!' Charlotte supposed it couldn't hurt just for today.

Edward chuckled. 'Gotcha. We had toast with peanut butter, and banana smoothies. Then we did some number games on the internet.'

So that's what they'd been up to. 'Isaac's homework?'

'Yes. He showed me the sheet that his teacher had given him. I found a game on the internet that made it a little bit more fun.'

'Thanks.' That feeling of dread she had when Edward did anything either for her or Isaac had almost completely disappeared now. Maybe because Edward so clearly enjoyed playing with Isaac.

'No trouble.' He buttered the toast and set it down in front of her, adding a jar of marmalade and one of apricot jam. Then coffee, hot and aromatic, with a dash of milk. Just one cup.

'I've got to go out...'

He was searching for his car keys and Charlotte pointed to the hook under the kitchen cabinet, where they were supposed to be.

'Right. Thanks. I'll be back shortly.'

'Shortly' could mean practically anything with Edward, and generally did. Charlotte opened her mouth to ask whether he'd be home for lunch, but he was already gone.

He returned an hour later, and appeared in the doorway between the hall and the living room carrying a long, thin parcel. He dumped it on the coffee table and sat down next to Charlotte on the sofa with an air of anticipation.

'What's that you're reading?' He craned over her shoulder, and Charlotte hugged the library book to her chest.

'Nothing... What's that you've got there?'

'Hmm...nothing.'

Another moment of quiet, and Charlotte returned to her book.

'Looks interesting. I haven't been there for ages.'

He was reading over her shoulder again, and Charlotte snapped the book shut.

'It's the summer holidays soon, and I thought I'd take Isaac out on a few daytrips. This book's got some really great ideas.' It seemed that—for the moment anyway—the plan that they should just get on with their lives without disturbing each other too much had gone by the board.

He grinned. 'The Natural History Museum's great for kids.'

'And for adults.' Charlotte had been looking for places which would interest her and Isaac—something that they could share—as well as a few fun places where he could work off his energy.

'And the Science Museum's just down the road, of course. There are some wonderful things there.'

'Yes.' He was going to be volunteering to come along any minute now, and the thought of Edward and Isaac together in the Science Museum sounded far too much like hard work. 'So what's in the parcel, then?'

'Ah! Thought you'd never ask.'

'So did I. Looks as if you've worn me down.'

She grinned at him and he was suddenly seized with motion, grasping the parcel and tearing the wrappings from it.

'What do you think?'

'It's a...' Isaac had run in from the garden and nosed his way in between them. 'What is it?'

'Here—see?' Edward pointed to the picture on the label. 'It's a kite.'

It wasn't just any old kite, but then Charlotte doubted that Edward would be much interested in anything that didn't have a complex structure of cords and an unlikely shape. He began to unwrap the collection of disassembled struts and sails, fishing out a small booklet.

Isaac watched open-mouthed and confused, looking to his mother for an explanation. 'Edward has to put all of those pieces together, sweetie, before it'll fly.'

'Yeah, shouldn't take long.' Edward was already laying the pieces out on the coffee table. 'Then we can go and fly it, eh, buddy?'

Charlotte left them to it and went to make drinks for them both. When she returned, Edward had already snapped into the fearsome concentration with which he approached almost any task, leaving Isaac shifting restlessly from one foot to the other. Charlotte placed his coffee on the table and he nodded absently.

'Thanks... Don't touch those, Isaac, I've put them all out in order.'

Isaac's hand shot away from the metal strut as if it had suddenly become red hot, and he hid it behind his back.

'Come here, sweetie.' Charlotte motioned her son towards her and put her arms around him. 'We'll just watch, shall we?'

Isaac nodded, obviously wishing that he could be a part of the construction project, craning to see what was happening. Edward seemed almost oblivious to the two of them, quickly selecting the pieces he wanted and deftly fitting them together.

They watched in silence. 'Look, sweetie, it's almost ready...' The structure was recognisable as a kite now, and Edward was attaching twine to the steering loops at each side.

Isaac nodded. But as Edward had worked she'd felt the excitement ebb out of her son's body, and now he was leaning against her legs with an air of boredom, his eyes on the television.

'Is it time for my programme, Mum?'

'Which programme, Isaac?'

'You know. *Eddie and the Magic Fish.*'

'Don't you want to wait until the kite's finished?'

'I want to see my programme.'

She saw the hurt in Edward's eyes. 'Okay. Come upstairs. You can see it there.'

There was a television in the guest bedroom, and perhaps it was best to let Isaac watch TV while Edward finished the kite. When they got to the point of flying it—and she was sure that Edward wouldn't be able to wait to try out the magnificent creation—Isaac's interest would be rekindled and everyone would be happy.

She left Isaac sprawled on her bed, clutching Stinky, captivated for the moment by the adventures of the Magic Fish. When she went back downstairs, the sitting room was empty. Charlotte could see Edward in the garden, ranging restlessly along the far end of the lawn, kicking at the inconsistencies in the smooth line between grass and flowerbeds.

Perhaps he needed to be left alone for a while, with his thoughts. He'd work it out; the mathematics weren't all that difficult. Isaac was five, and there were times when Edward's focussed ardour for the task in hand simply left him behind.

But there were elements to this equation that intellect, even one as all-consuming as Edward's, couldn't grasp. Twisting her mouth, and in defiance of all that was logical, Charlotte slipped through the open French windows and walked across the grass towards him.

He was lost in his thoughts, seeming not to notice her. 'Given up, then?' She might as well start with a challenge, if that was the way she meant to go on.

'The kite's finished.'

'Yes, I saw that.'

He turned to her, giving her a speculative look, as if he was trying to weigh the situation up. 'He didn't like the kite. That's okay. Isaac's free to have his own likes and dislikes...'

'Edward, did you ever go to school?'

He blinked at her, struggling to make the connection. 'As it happens, no. By the time I was five I'd already got a handle on calculus and my parents had me tutored at home.'

There was a note of sadness in his voice.

'That must have been lonely.'

He shrugged. 'I don't have anything to compare it with.'

'When everything's fine, you don't need anything to compare it with.'

There was something dull in his eyes as he focussed on her. 'You're saying I don't play well with others.' One hand clenched into a fist. 'That's not exactly an original thought.'

He just wasn't listening to her. It was as if it had been drilled into Edward that being clever meant that you didn't have a heart. 'Maybe it's just a self-fulfilling prophecy. If you believe it's true, then ultimately it is.'

He glared at her. 'And you have a better idea?'

He turned, as if the conversation was now at an end. He was used to having the last word. Used to being right.

'Don't be so arrogant...' Even before he turned back she knew that she'd missed the mark by about a mile. Edward might look and sound arrogant, but somewhere beneath that there was a lonely child.

'I am what I am, Charlotte. If you want to think that's arrogant, then go right ahead.'

All of his defences were up now. The aloof, unsmiling man, whom no one seemed to be able to get close to, was turning away from her again.

She did the unthinkable. Marched straight up to

him and grabbed his arm, pulling him around to face her. 'You don't fool me, Edward. I've seen you with Isaac. I saw you with Mercy the other day.'

Something behind his eyes ignited. Dark blue ice turning to sparkling heat. There was more than enough emotion here. It was just a matter of whether she could deal with it. Whether *Edward* could deal with it, without ducking back into the comfort of his books.

'Mercy opened up to you, not me.'

'Edward! Sometimes I want to shake some sense into you...!'

The provocative twitch of his lips told her that she could go right ahead, if that was her inclination, and she resisted the urge.

'What on earth happened to you when you were a child?'

'You think I was a poor little bright boy, with his nose in a book and no friends? It wasn't like that.' He pursed his lips. 'Not quite like that, anyway.'

'What *was* it like, then?'

'I was different. By the time I was ten I could keep up with a university undergraduate on an intellectual level. On a social level, I wasn't quite ready for women, all-night parties and beer-drinking contests. It was difficult to find my own space.'

'You felt out of step, you mean? Your emotions and theirs?'

He looked at her gravely. Then suddenly he smiled. 'Most people assume I don't have any emotions.'

His look taunted her. Dared her to tell him different.

'That's not true, though, is it?' She dared him back.

'I don't think so.'

The dare turned dangerous all of a sudden. He was waiting for her to kiss him. Charlotte baulked at that one.

'Look, Edward, I know that you're used to being better and faster at everything than everyone else, and that it's a lot easier to do things by yourself. But if you want Isaac to be interested in what you're doing then you have to slow down a bit and do things at his pace.'

He hesitated. 'I'm…not very good at that. As you can see.'

'No one's born good at things like that—you have to learn. You're supposed to be a genius. Can't you learn? Or don't you want to learn?'

'I want to.' The admission was a little stiff, and left Edward nonplussed for a moment. 'Why don't you go and tell Isaac…?'

She glared at him and he grinned.

'Why don't I go and tell him myself?'

'Good idea.'

'Right.' He clapped his hands together, as if he was about to embark on one of the most complex experiments of his life. 'Do you think he'd like his own kite? One that's more his size, perhaps?'

Charlotte almost told him no, that Isaac didn't need a kite. But she knew he'd want one, and Edward needed this.

'I think he'd love that. Go and ask him.'

Edward didn't deal in half-measures. The shop he took them to sold nothing but kites, and on a bright late summer's morning, was full of people. He led Isaac straight to a selection of different coloured children's kites, and the two of them became immediately absorbed in sorting through them. Charlotte decided to leave them to it.

'I'm just going to pop to the chemist, to buy some soap. I won't be long. Stay here with Edward, won't you, Isaac?' She nudged his shoulder with her hand.

Isaac ignored her in favour of the kites, and Edward looked up at her. He seemed to know how hard it always was for her to leave Isaac, even for a few minutes, and he took hold of the boy's hand as a gesture of intent.

'I won't let him out of my sight. Go and do your shopping.'

She decided to take her time, to give Edward and Isaac a chance to buy the kite by themselves. There were some nice apples on display outside the greengrocer's and she stopped to buy three, to go with the packed lunch in the boot of the car.

In the chemist's she ran her finger along the lines of jars and bottles which were beyond her purchasing power, now.

Her old soap, the one she'd used to buy before she'd begun to make all her decisions on the basis of price, was there. Something from her old life, when she hadn't needed to question every word, every action, every penny that she spent. She so wanted that back.

Charlotte picked it up, hesitated, put it back on the shelf, then picked it up again.

It wouldn't matter if she had something that she wanted for once. The soap smelled nice and felt creamy on her skin, and it wasn't so very much more expensive than the more economical brands. As luxuries went, this wasn't so very ostentatious.

'Come on, Mum…' Isaac broke into the debate, tugging at her arm.

She looked round to see Edward, with a firm hold on Isaac's other hand to prevent any possible escape.

'Okay, just a minute. Did you get your kite?' It was clear that he had, Edward was holding a large plastic bag.

'Yes, do you want to see?'

'Mmm. Yes, please.'

Isaac grinned up at Edward, who delivered the bag into his grasp. Inside was a small blue kite with a blue and silver tail.

'Oh, that's so pretty!' She drew the kite out to examine its tail. 'Those sparkly bits are going to shine in the sun when you fly it.'

Isaac nodded, carefully showing her everything. There was a ball of twine, mounted on a reel, to protect Isaac's hands from any friction. 'You tie it on there—see?' Isaac indicated the reinforced eyelets on the kite. 'With a special knot.'

Charlotte nodded, impressed. 'A special knot, eh?'

'Yes. Edward's going to show me how,' Isaac responded proudly.

Her little boy was growing up. It was almost a

surprise to find that she didn't mind that Isaac wanted Edward to help him tie the knots on his precious kite, when it felt only a blink of time since her son had looked to her for everything.

'That's great. Make sure you watch what he does carefully.'

'Can we go, Mum?' Isaac was impatient again, jigging up and down on the spot.

'Yes, let me get my soap and we'll be off.' Charlotte looked up to see Edward, in a world of his own, working his way along the shelf and inspecting the ingredients lists printed on all the soap wrappers. 'Edward?'

He jolted back into the here and now. 'Ah. Yes.' He focussed on the soap in her hand and took a matching bar from the shelf. 'That one smells nice.'

She didn't really need it. The thought that Edward liked the smell of it made her want it, though. 'They're all much the same. I'll get this one.' She put the bar back onto the shelf and reached for the cheaper brand.

'I imagine they're all pretty easy to make...' He still had one foot in that world of possibilities that seemed to know no bounds. He inspected the bar in his hand. 'Pretty standard ingredients.'

'*You* might be able to make it. *I'd* probably blow the kitchen up. It's just soap, Edward.' Nothing was just anything to Edward. Everything fascinated him, from pizza-making to nuclear physics. When she was with him the world seemed bigger, far more interesting.

'Hmm. You like this one, though?' He still had the bar that he'd taken from the shelf in his hand.

'This will do. It's cheaper.'

Before she could reach into her bag for her purse Edward had given her preferred choice to Isaac, along with a note from his pocket. 'You want to get it for your mum?'

She met his gaze. This wasn't anything to do with kites, or soap. It was about whether she had the right to a treat, however small. Whether Edward had the right to give it to her, to claim a place in their little family.

'Okay. Thank you.'

He nodded, grinning.

'At last!' Isaac conferred his displeasure on both of them and ran to the counter.

Charlotte watched as the woman at the cash desk smiled down at Isaac, took his money and put the soap into a bag, counting his change into his hand.

'Hey! Hey, give Edward his change back.' Isaac had pocketed the coins.

'That's okay.' Edward winked at her. 'He might be needing it later for ice-cream.'

Isaac looked from Charlotte to Edward, then back again, waiting to obtain a final decision. 'All right, then. Here—let me zip your pocket up, so you don't lose it.'

She bent and fastened Isaac's pocket, then gave way to the pressure from both Edward and Isaac and hurried with them to the car. The afternoon was bright and blustery, just right for kite-flying, and the three of them seemed in complete accord. No one wanted to miss a moment of it.

CHAPTER ELEVEN

THEY DROVE FOR an hour, right out of London, making a beeline for high ground. The last five hundred yards had to be walked—or rather climbed—until finally they reached the exact location that Edward wanted.

'It's windy enough here.' The words were almost dragged away on the breeze as soon as they left her mouth.

'Yes. I think this will do.' Edward looked around with an air of satisfaction. 'Which kite shall we try first?'

'The big one!' Isaac was jumping up and down with excitement. 'I want to see the big one...'

'Okay.' Edward grinned, laying the large kite onto the ground, clipping together the last pieces of the framework so that it was ready to fly. 'You see, I think that the wind will catch it here...' he indicated the breadth of the kite '...and funnel through this way...' A sweep of the hand to show the anticipated wind direction. 'That should give it extra lift, and the weight of the tail makes it steadier.' He grinned. 'That's the theory, anyway.'

'Will it work?' Isaac stamped his foot impatiently.

'That's what we're here to find out. It's all very well to have a theory, but you always have to test it out... Here, you hang on there.'

Edward gave the kite to Isaac and winked at Charlotte, walking away from them as he unravelled the twin reels of lightweight cord.

He paced out the distance and called back to Isaac, 'Okay, hold it up...'

Charlotte kept a discreet hold on the top of the kite, in case Isaac decided to let go of it before he was supposed to.

'Now, on my count... One...two...three...let her go!'

The kite rose in a straight line, up into the clear blue sky. Isaac shouted at the top of his voice in excitement, and suddenly the only thing to do was to shout with him.

'Nooooo!' The kite dipped erratically and Isaac screamed in horror.

Edward fought for control for long moments and then the kite soared upwards again. Charlotte cheered, and Isaac followed suit, running towards Edward.

'That didn't quite work...' Edward was grinning at her. 'Perhaps I'll just concentrate on keeping it up there at this stage.'

'I want to hold it... Pleeeease...' Isaac was pulling at Charlotte's windcheater in excitement.

'I don't think so, sweetie. It's very hard to control. We don't want you flying away with the kite.'

'Owww.' Isaac seemed to think that flying away was an added bonus.

'What about yours?' Edward reeled his kite in and turned his attention to Isaac's blue and silver kite.

Isaac's face was a picture. Happiness that he was a part of their great enterprise and not just relegated to watching. Pride when the kite soared up into the sky, with Edward kneeling at his side, showing him how to control it.

'Thank you.' Charlotte caught at his sleeve as he stepped back, letting Isaac go solo. 'Thank you so much.'

Edward nodded in satisfaction. 'Every boy needs a kite. I'm just going to make a few adjustments to mine and perhaps you'll help me launch it again.'

A few knots, a little staring into the middle distance as Edward estimated airflow and wind speed, and the kite was up in the air again, this time flying more steadily. Charlotte ran back to Edward's side and he looped his arms over her head.

'Here, you try. Take hold of the reels.'

She pressed her hands over his, trying to stop her fingers from trembling. The wind around them buffeted her, but she was safe in his arms, her back against his strong body, his scent surrounding her and then blown away by the wind.

'That's right.'

His lips were almost touching her ear.

'Pull it a bit to the right.' He guided her arm and the kite dipped to the right, shooting back upwards as the breeze caught it again. 'Ooops. Hang on tight.'

Suddenly he had left her, and was loping across to Isaac, who was struggling to keep his kite in the air.

Charlotte concentrated hard on controlling her own little bit of airspace while Edward restored Isaac's kite safely back above their heads. He made sure that Isaac was happily in control again and then he was back.

'What do you think?' He was surveying the flight path of the kite.

'It's pulling really hard...' Her arms were already beginning to ache.

Edward chuckled, looping his arms around her again. 'Let me give you a hand with it.'

He wasn't helping at all. All that happened was that she melted into his arms, turning to jelly and losing whatever strength she had left. He was controlling not only the kite but her as well. She let go of the kite strings and he strengthened his grip, catching them just in time. Turning in his arms, she faced him.

His rakish half-smile told her that this was just what he wanted. 'Giving up already?'

'You're so much better at it than I am.'

'Think so? You dip beautifully.' He leaned towards her.

She couldn't do this. Not with Isaac just yards away—even if he was paying them no attention.

She ducked out of the circle of his arms, feeling the wind suddenly chill her. 'Are you hungry?'

Edward chuckled. 'Ravenous.'

She fixed him with a glare. Even the thought of Peter's quiet charm, and the way that had worked out, wasn't enough to calm the insistent thunder in her veins. Peter was like a faded shadow of a man next to Edward. Edward was different. Different from pretty much everyone she'd ever met.

'Would you like an apple?' She gritted her teeth and doggedly refused to take any notice of the alternative interpretation of hungry that the curve of his eyebrow suggested.

'In a minute. I've got my hands full at the moment.' His gaze left her, flipping over towards Isaac. 'Steady on, there, chief...'

Charlotte ran to her son, helping him to pull on the string so that the kite fluttered upwards again. 'Enjoying yourself, sweetie?' She whispered the words tremulously in his ear.

'Yes, Mum.' Isaac's attention was on the kite, its tail shimmering and sparkling in the sunshine. He submitted to a hug for a moment and then wriggled free.

'Good. I'm glad.'

She could have cried. The scared little boy who had clung to her when the debt collectors knocked on the door was gone. In his place a child who was enjoying himself so much that he had no time for his mother's cuddles.

'All right over there?' Edward nodded over to Isaac.

'Just fine. He loves this.'
'Yeah. Me, too.'

Edward sat at the piano, his fingers wandering across the keys, playing a soft melody of his own composition. He'd had a great time. The kite had flown better than he'd expected once he'd made a few adjustments to the lines which had altered its angle of flight slightly. Isaac had liked his kite, too, and had insisted on taking it to bed with him. And Charlotte...

He'd planned to give her a great day—help her forget about the troubles of the past week. And she'd shone in the sunshine like a beautiful jewel, full of life and light. But however hard he tried to please her he seemed to end up only pleasing himself, as the echoes of her *joie de vivre* washed over him.

Charlotte. The chords seemed to sing out her name. A sudden slip into a minor key lent an element of yearning to the music that hadn't been there before.

'Why so sad?'

He hadn't noticed her behind him, standing in the doorway which led from the kitchen. He stopped playing abruptly, aware that the music had given away much more than he had ever intended. 'It's a slow piece of music.'

A slight frown of disbelief. It seemed that he could lie to the rest of the world, but Charlotte caught him out every time.

'I recognise it. You've played it before.'

When he'd played it before it had been just a dalliance with the keys. Now it was a full-blown, passionate love affair, full of all the conflicting emotions in his heart. 'It's a work in progress. It changes every time.'

She nodded. Walked over to him. 'Will you play it again?'

'No.' She couldn't lure him in like that. If the music insisted on betraying him, then he'd stick to other people's compositions. 'I mean…I need to think about it a bit more.'

She nodded and he beckoned her over. This time she sat down next to him on the piano stool as if it was the most natural thing in the world.

'Would you like something else?'

'If you want.' She smiled. 'Whatever you want.'

'Your turn to choose.'

She grinned. 'What was it you were playing the other night?' She hummed a few chords, her voice clear and tuneful.

'You've got a good ear. Most people don't get that bit right.' He reproduced the chords she'd sung and she smiled, singing along with the music.

He'd played this song thousands of times before. Kathy had liked this one, too, but it had never felt like this. Never as if he was caressing someone with the music. Never so head-swimmingly erotic.

He hadn't thought about Kathy in years. If asked, he would have said that he'd forgotten her, but it seemed that she'd just lain dormant in his memory, waiting to emerge and reprimand him for having ignored the lesson she'd taught him.

'What's the matter?'

Charlotte was closer now, and Edward realised that he'd stopped playing.

He shrugged. 'This song reminds me of…someone I used to know.'

'Should I be sorry?'

He shook his head. 'I don't think so. It was a long time ago. When I was at university.'

'Which time?'

'The second. Kathy was a medical student.'

She nodded. 'First love?'

He shrugged. 'I suppose so.'

It had been more like a first friendship, really. Kathy had been quiet, studious, so like him that everyone had reckoned they were made for each other and it was just a matter of time before they got married.

When she'd left him, citing a lack of emotional commitment on Edward's part as her reason, it had been proof positive to all their friends that Edward was the cold fish they'd always marked him down as being.

She nodded. 'My first love was Isaac's father. That didn't work out too well.'

'But you loved him once...' The words almost choked Edward.

'You know they say that love is blind?' She looked up at him and he nodded. 'Well, I don't think so. I think that real love sees everything.'

'Do you think you can really ever see everything about someone?'

'I don't know. In the absence of any substantive evidence either way, I'll have to say that it's just a theory. But they say that true love lasts, and I don't love him now.' Her mouth twisted, as if the joke was really on her.

Something inside him raged in bitter triumph. The impulse to tear Charlotte's ex limb from limb de-escalated to wanting to give him a more minor, if acutely painful, set of injuries. If she didn't care about him any more then Edward could live with that.

'You can't regret all of it. Isaac...'

'Isaac's the best thing that ever happened to me.' She laid a finger on his shoulder, as if alerting him to something. 'Good things do come from bad.'

'If you make them.'

Charlotte had that ability. As for himself... Nothing good or bad had come from his time with Kathy. Just a lingering doubt about whether he really could ever commit to anyone. After everything that had happened today that doubt suddenly seemed to matter a great deal.

She was looking steadily at him. That silent interrogation which he found so difficult to withstand. Why didn't she just *ask*?

'How long were you and Kathy together?'

'Three years.'

She nodded. Seemed to be about to ask more, and then didn't. That was as well, really. The nagging feeling of failure whenever Kathy's name was mentioned made him uncomfortable.

'So we're two of a kind, then.' She gave a little sigh.

'What makes you say that?' Charlotte was warm, bubbly—everyone knew without even thinking about it that there was nothing she didn't know about emotional commitment.

'Both still waiting for the right one to come along.'

It felt as if the right one was sitting next to him. But that must be another mistake, because Charlotte clearly didn't think so.

'No. I'm not waiting.' Edward told himself, with less conviction than normal, that he had everything he needed. His work, his books. The textured, multicoloured, harmonic flow of the world around him, perfect in all its intricacies.

'Better watch out, then.'

He was aware that her gaze was on him.

'Why?'

'That's when things sneak up on you from behind. When you least expect them.'

He turned to tell her that she was wrong—one smooth movement which began with a shake of his head, and ended with her lips. She gave a little start of surprise and then... Then she kissed him back.

Soft...slow.

Edward was taking it gently, giving her every opportunity to draw back from him, but that was the very last thing that Charlotte wanted to do.

When he brushed his fingers against her neck, his thumb caressing her jaw, she felt her breath quicken.

He was all for the moment. Each touch was special and not to be rushed. Every breath was one they wouldn't take again, unique and remarkable. His fingertips found hers, touching, sensing, and then wrapping around her hand, drawing it upwards. Holding her gaze, he brushed his lips against the back of her fingers.

There was more. Simmering beneath the surface. Waiting. He took the pace up a notch, just one, his hand on the nape of her neck, pulling her in for another kiss. This time there was an edge to it, a promise of so much more if she could only stand this long, slow preamble.

He didn't call out her name. Made no profession of desire, or love, or even friendship. He didn't need to. It was all there in his kiss, the heat banking and flaring until she felt herself begin to tremble.

They broke apart. Charlotte's heart was thudding in her chest, her lungs pulling in air.

'Does that make any difference?' he asked.

'What do you mean?' Of course it made a difference. Edward's kiss made all the difference in the world. Fear clutched at her.

'I mean does that make you or me into different people? Change any of our views on life?'

She wished it did, but all of the old doubts were still there, the dread that she might fall back into disaster again. 'No.'

'Then I guess we'll say that there's someone out there for you, and someone for me. Leave it at that.'

So this was the way he wanted to play it. Just a kiss between friends. *Like hell it was.* That had been the first step on a path which led straight to two naked bodies and mind-blowing sex. They needed no words to know that.

He was right, though. Sex with Edward, if she ever managed to survive the intensity of the fore-play, would be like jumping from the frying pan into a searing fire. She couldn't afford to be fooled again by quiet charm and hidden depths. She wanted—needed—everything to be in plain sight.

'Yes. That would probably be sensible.' It seemed almost wrong to stand up now. Like the biggest lie of all to deny what had just happened. But she did it. 'I'm going to...'

Saying that she was going to bed would sound

like a come-on. And his gaze was still so very enticing. Charlotte was under no illusions about whether she would be able to say no to him if he reached out for her now.

His slow smile was laced with all of the intentions that neither of them seemed able to follow through on. 'I'll leave you to it.'

'Thank you.'

What was that for? Starting things? Stopping things?

She leaned forward and planted a kiss on his cheek, drawing back again. 'Goodnight. I'll see you in the morning.'

CHAPTER TWELVE

IT HAD OCCURRED to Edward to burst into her room, carry her off to his, and make love to her until the raging in his blood let up. That might well have been a long and exhausting process, but that wasn't what had stopped him. It was what came afterwards—the falling in love and realising that he couldn't give her what she needed.

He was older now, and perhaps a bit wiser. He'd seen more of the world. Met Charlotte. Maybe things could be different. But *maybe* wasn't a good enough word for someone like Charlotte.

No emotional commitment. The words on Kathy's lips had puzzled and upset him. If he dared to make love to Charlotte, then those words on her lips might just kill him.

So he wouldn't. Instead he'd carry on as normal.

More or less normal, anyway.

It was with a pang of unusual regret that he rose from the kitchen table at seven the following morning and began to scribble a note for her, saying that he was going to catch up on some work he had to do at the Hunter Clinic and wouldn't be in for lunch.

'You're up early.'

Her bright morning smile interrupted him, almost choking him with desire.

'You, too.' The house was still quiet, and Edward wondered whether he'd made a mistake in not following his instincts last night. If Isaac was asleep, there was still time...

'Oh, I've just taken the opportunity to come down and make some sandwiches. Isaac's playing in his room. He'll be racing around wanting to get dressed soon.'

'Ah. I'll leave you to it, then...' It looked as if the Hunter Clinic was his best bet after all.

'We're going to the park this morning. Some of Isaac's friends go boating on the lake on Sundays. I'll leave you a salad for lunch...'

'There's no need...'

'Or you could come with us if you'd like?'

Charlotte, Isaac and Edward. Almost as if they were a family.

Edward picked up the note he'd been writing, screwed it into a ball and dropped it into the kitchen wastebin. 'Yes, I'm at a loose end today. That would be nice.'

The summer sunshine sparkled on the water like diamonds swept up from the bed of the lake in the wake of the small boats which bobbed on its surface.

'Mum... Mum, they're already here. Quick!'

Isaac was running back and forth, trying to hasten the easy pace which she and Edward had fallen into.

'There's plenty of time. Don't you want to go and find Sam first?' Sam was Isaac's best friend from school. 'Look, there he is.' Charlotte waved to Sam's mother and Isaac ran off across the grass, leaving her and Edward to follow in their own time.

'It's a nice day for it.' Edward was surveying the water.

'Yes. It gets a bit crowded sometimes on Sunday afternoons, but if you come before lunch and bring a picnic—' Charlotte broke off, shading her eyes against the glare. 'What are those two boys up to?'

A small boat was rocking precariously as two boys in their early teens took it into their heads to start a mock- fight in the deepest part of the lake. One caught the other with a flailing fist and they both crashed into the water, the boat rocking wildly and threatening to capsize.

'Edward...' She caught his arm and then started to breathe again as two heads bobbed to the surface of the lake and the boys started to doggy paddle towards shallower water. 'Those kids— they could have hurt themselves... Where's the attendant?'

Heads turned as the park attendant jumped into a boat, quickly pushing off towards the boys. Then a shrill wail floated across the still air.

'What's that...?' Charlotte scanned the water and located the source of the scream. She'd thought that the boys were alone in the boat, but there was also a shock of blonde curls just visible inside of the boat. 'Sit down!' she screamed at the child, even though it was unlikely that her voice would carry that far, much less be heeded.

The child managed to get to her feet and the boat bucked wildly.

'Edward, she's going to fall in...'

Her words met thin air. The bag he'd been carrying lay where he'd dropped it, and Edward was already powering down the steep slope which led to the lake, throwing off his jacket and shoes. By the time the other adults gathered around the lake started to notice the little girl he was already wading into the water, then swimming towards the child with long, easy strokes.

The little girl had calmed down now, and it seemed as if he would soon reach her. Charlotte glanced quickly in Isaac's direction and saw that Sam's mother had both him and Sam firmly in her grasp, stopping them both from running down to the lake's edge.

Edward was nearly there. Only another fifty yards.

It was fifty yards too much.

The wake from another boat made the craft wobble and the child screamed again, panicking, throwing herself from one side to the other. The boat capsized, taking her with it.

No time for the curse of disbelief which sprang to her lips. Charlotte ran to the waterside, one eye still on Isaac. Sam's mother shouted a reassurance that she'd look after him and Charlotte hitched up her skirt and began to wade into the water.

Edward had reached the spot where the upturned boat lay in the water and was looking around for the child.

'Edward... She's under the water.'

He didn't turn his head, but he must have heard. His body seemed to rise in the water, and then disappeared as he dived beneath the surface.

Long moments.

The water was almost opaque here at the edge of the lake, and Charlotte could only hope that it was a bit clearer further out. He had to find her.

How long was it now? Thirty seconds? A minute? Charlotte knew that Edward wouldn't come back up until he'd found the child, and prayed that it would be soon.

The surface of the lake erupted in a frenzy of bubbles and water as Edward broke the surface. He struck out immediately for the shore, not stopping to take a breath although his lungs must have been screaming for air. As soon as the water was shallow enough he gained a footing and waded, the little girl clinging tightly to his neck.

For a moment all Charlotte could feel was relief. Water was sluicing from Edward's chest and legs and the child moved in his arms, leaving a watery red stain on the shoulder of his white shirt.

'Edward...' She waded further into the water, meeting him as he strode towards the bank. 'You're bleeding...'

'It's not my blood.' He nodded quickly towards the little girl, who was whimpering now, holding on tight to his shirt collar. 'Clear a space for me, will you?'

Charlotte stumbled, splashing up onto the bank. 'Some space, please, guys. My friend's a doctor—give him some space.'

Two women assumed the responsibility of moving everyone back, and someone threw a waterproof sheet down onto the ground. Edward dropped to his knees, ready to examine the child, but she wouldn't let go of him.

'All right, honey. You're such a brave girl, and you're safe now. Let me look at your arm...'

He gently tried to move the child and she hung on even tighter. Charlotte could see a gash on her forearm, which was gushing blood.

'Okay. That's okay.'

Charlotte expected him to use his vastly superior strength to free himself, but instead he held the child closer, motioning to Charlotte.

'Looks as if you're going to have to look at her arm *in situ*...'

Charlotte dropped to her knees next to him, gently lifting the little girl's arm. 'She's got a nasty cut, and it's bleeding badly. She'll definitely need to go to hospital.' She looked up, and almost simultaneously half a dozen mobile phones appeared.

'We'll just need the one ambulance.' She grinned at the knot of people around them. 'Are her parents here?'

Sam's mother's voice sounded above the general hubbub. 'Dave, call an ambulance. Everyone else—see if you can find her mother. Who are those boys she was with...?'

Charlotte left Maggie to it, with only the briefest glance in her direction to check that she was still holding firmly onto Isaac's hand.

'I'm going to have to wrap something around her arm to stop the bleeding.'

'All right.'

The little girl screamed as Charlotte gently wrapped her own scarf around the wound, pressing firmly and extending the arm upwards.

'It's okay, honey. I know it hurts, but you're all right.' Edward's voice was almost painfully gentle, and the screams subsided to a whimper. 'You're doing really well.'

She couldn't tell whether the child understood his words, or his manner. Whichever it was, she was beginning to calm.

'What's your name, sweetie?' Edward managed to disentangle himself sufficiently to ask the question face to face, rather than direct it at the top of the child's head.

'Laura.'

'Well, Laura, you're safe now. I expect your arm hurts, but we'll put a bandage around it and it'll be better in no time.'

Laura nodded up at him. It occurred to Charlotte that she might like to remind Edward of his own words on the subject of his ability to communicate with patients, and she promised herself she'd do it later. He might not want to admit to being so very wrong in front of all these people.

'What happened? She was under the water for a very long time...' Charlotte had half expected to see Edward bring Laura up unconscious.

He grinned at her. 'She instinctively did just the right thing. When the boat capsized she ended up in an air pocket underneath it, and she held on to one of the seats. The biggest problem was getting her to let go of it and hang on to me instead.' His free hand patted Laura's back. 'You've got a great grip, there, young lady.'

Laura looked up at him, favouring him with a tremulous smile. At that moment the knot of people around them parted as a woman came stumbling through.

'Laura...' The woman fell to her knees in front of Edward. 'Laura, I'm so sorry... Is she all right? They said you're a doctor...'

'She's okay.' Edward delivered Laura into her mother's arms while Charlotte kept a tight hold on her arm. 'She has a cut on her arm, and needs to keep it elevated until the ambulance arrives. She'll need a few stitches, but the main thing is that she didn't stop breathing.'

'Laura...' The mother held her daughter tight, her eyes squeezed closed.

Charlotte knew just what scenes were playing in her head. She'd had her own share of them with Isaac recently.

'It's fine. You have a very resourceful young lady for a daughter, there.'

The woman's eyes opened and tears spilled from them. 'I only left her for a minute... The kids wanted ice-cream and I told Trevor to look after her.' One of the boys who had been fighting in the boat stood beside her, soaking wet, bedraggled, and not a little shamefaced.

'She's fine. That's the main thing. Her head was only under the water for a few moments—'

He broke off as tears coursed down the woman's cheeks. Someone proffered a handkerchief, but she wouldn't let go of her daughter for long enough to wipe her eyes.

Edward turned to Charlotte. 'How's that cut doing?'

'I think it's stopped bleeding.' She loosened her grip on Laura's arm and blood began to seep between her fingers. 'Ah. Not quite.'

'Okay. Can the ambulance get to us here?'

'Yes, the park gates are wide enough for them to get through, and they can use the service road that runs through the park, right there.'

He nodded. 'Good. We'll just sit tight here, then.'

The paramedic from the ambulance returned Charlotte's scarf to her with a wry smile. 'Try washing it in cold water...'

'Thanks.' Charlotte took the scarf. Hot water would only fix the bloodstain and it would never come out. Cold water might do the trick.

'I should have offered to rip my shirt up for a bandage.' Edward's voice sounded behind her. 'It's already ruined.'

Ruined it might be, and bloodstained and dirty

from the lake, clinging to his shoulders and chest in the places where the sun hadn't dried it, but it was still better on than off. Marginally. When he'd emerged from the water the white lawn fabric had left very little to the imagination.

'Probably best you keep it.' She grinned up at him. 'We don't want to get all the mothers talking. I have to face them at the school gates, remember.'

He gave her a hurt look. 'I'm allowed to rip up my shirt for bandages, aren't I? I thought it was practically par for the course when a doctor has to improvise.'

'Only when there's nothing else to use. I'm a nurse, remember, and I had a scarf handy.'

'Hmm. Shame to spoil it, though.' He caught the end of the fine material through his fingers. 'It's pretty.'

It was her favourite. It went with her blouse, and she'd chosen both from her wardrobe this morning because they were a little smarter than the T-shirts she usually wore at the weekend. If she had allowed herself to examine her motives for that choice she would have had to admit that Edward had played a major part in it.

'It'll wash out.'

'Hmm. You've got a spot of blood on your cuff, as well.'

'That'll wash out, too.' Charlotte rolled the sleeves of her blouse up a little, to hide the stain.

'Yeah. Look, I'll take it home with me and put it in a bowl of cold water. Sam's father...'

'Dave?'

'Yeah, Dave. He's offered to run me home to get a change of clothes. We'll only be half an hour.'

'You'll be coming back?'

'Of course. We haven't eaten our picnic yet.' Edward watched as Laura's mother climbed into the ambulance, shepherding her son with her. 'His ears are going to be ringing tonight.'

'I imagine so.' It was so easy. You only had to take your eye off them for one minute...Charlotte shook her head.

'Isaac's okay.' He pointed towards Sam and Isaac, playing together in the grass under Maggie's watchful eye.

'Yeah, I know.' Still she couldn't help the terrible feeling of foreboding.

'I can understand your fears. With everything that's happened. But no one's going to let anything happen to him.'

'No.' She had to be content with that. With

Edward's promises, his father's reassurances. 'Look, you're shivering. You must be freezing.' His hair and shirt were beginning to dry, but Edward's jeans were still soaking wet.

He shrugged. 'I could do with getting those dry clothes. Will you be okay here with Isaac?'

'Yes, fine. See you later.'

He grinned. 'I wouldn't miss this afternoon for the world.'

Charlotte sat with Maggie on the grass, hugging her knees in front of her.

'So, Edward's...a friend of yours...?'

'Yes, I work with him.'

'Ah. A colleague. Well, it was lucky he was here today. He was a real hero.' Maggie laughed. 'I told Isaac and Sam that I thought he was a hero, and Isaac asked if that made him a hero, too. Since Edward was his friend.'

Charlotte grinned at the thought. 'What did you say?'

'I said that it did. Then Sam wanted to know if he was a hero, too, as he was Isaac's friend...'

'I reckon it's catching, this hero business.'

'Definitely.' Maggie leaned towards Charlotte confidingly. 'Mind you, even my heart skipped a beat when he walked out of the water carrying that little girl.'

'Yeah?'

Charlotte's heart had almost stopped. Edward's jeans, moulded tight around his strong thighs... His shirt clinging to a broad, muscled chest which had been heaving from the effort of getting to Laura in time and pulling her from the lake... The droplets of spinning silver that had scattered as he shook his head... It was an image that she wasn't going to forget in a hurry.

'Guess mine did, too.'

'It's instinct. Man saves child. Guaranteed to pull at the heartstrings.'

Head, heart and all points south. If Laura hadn't been the most pressing priority she would have had little choice but to fling herself into his arms.

'Yeah.' She turned to Maggie with a bright smile. 'And it all ended well.'

'Yep. Thanks to you two.' Maggie lay back in the grass. 'I think it's going to be a great afternoon.'

'So, if you ever tell me again that you're no good at reassuring patients...'

Charlotte was grinning at him, as if she knew

that Edward was expecting something of the sort from her. At least she'd left it until Isaac was safely tucked up in bed.

'Okay.' He looked up from his book, holding his hands up in mock surrender. 'You just had to say it, didn't you?' But it had felt good to be the one who gave comfort for a change. He could see the extra dimension that it added to Charlotte's job.

She laughed. 'Do you mind?'

'No. I'd mind if you hadn't noticed.'

Charlotte's approval was becoming more important to him than he was strictly comfortable with. It was one thing to gain satisfaction from trying out a new approach and finding that it worked, but that didn't mean that he'd changed. He might be older, and a bit wiser, but were Kathy's words so very wide of the mark?

She jutted her chin at him. 'So you admit that you've underestimated yourself?'

The phone interrupted any possible answer to that, and Edward reached for the handset. He heard his father's voice, with a quick enquiry about how he was doing and a request to speak to Charlotte.

'Here.' He spun the handset across the coffee

table and she caught it adroitly. 'It's my father. He wants to speak to you.'

He couldn't have asked for a better illustration of Kathy's point. Even his father seemed to be captivated with her, and somehow found far more to chat about with Charlotte than he did with Edward.

He retreated into a book, hardly hearing what Charlotte was saying on the phone. After half an hour she replaced the handset into its cradle.

'Everything okay?'

'He wanted to set up a meeting for this week. I'm going to see him on Wednesday, after work. He's got some things for me to sign.'

'Good. Anything else?' That would have accounted for about two minutes' worth of their conversation.

'He asked me if I knew anything about the different cuts you can get on precious stones.'

'Really? Do you?'

She nodded. 'My father was a jeweller. The old-fashioned kind, who knew how to make pieces as well as sell them. So I know a little.'

'I imagine he's got their fortieth wedding anniversary in mind—that's only a few months away now.' Edward wondered whether he should follow his father's lead and enlist Charlotte's help in choosing a gift for his parents.

'Mmm. He wants to get something really special. I'm going to give him the name of an associate of my father's who deals in rubies when I see him. He does very fine work. I used to have a necklace that he made for my mother.'

Her voice was matter-of-fact. Just the smallest hint of regret.

'Used to have?' Edward hoped against all reason that the necklace was somewhere tucked away safely—the one thing that Charlotte hadn't sold.

'I sold it. It gave me a few thousand to put towards the deposit on my house.'

'I'm sorry you had to do that.'

She shrugged. 'They're only pretty sparkly things. I remember my parents, and that's the thing that really matters.' She pulled her shoulders back, as if telling herself for the hundredth time that it really didn't matter. 'Anyway, I know a good ruby when I see one. I'll make sure that your father gets a really nice stone.'

'Thank you.' She was quite unselfish in her generosity. Even though she'd lost everything herself, she wanted to make sure that another woman had the perfect gift. 'So, do you need someone to look after Isaac on Wednesday evening?'

'I can have the childminder pick him up from school. That's what I usually do.'

'I've got a free afternoon. I can pick him up and bring him back here if you like.'

She nodded. 'If it's not too much trouble. I don't want to...'

'If you were going to say that you don't want to impose, you can save your breath.' He kept the stern glare up for about two seconds, until she flushed and it melted. 'You're not imposing. It's been a pleasure having him around.'

She grinned, a hint of mischief in her eyes. He could get lost in that mischief, let it bend and break him...

'You two are getting to be quite a gang...'

'Yeah?' Edward had never been in a gang before, even if this was an exceptionally small one. He quite liked the possibilities that it opened up. Going fishing for tadpoles. Wearing their ties like bandanas around their heads.

'I just... Well, I hope that he's not been too demanding. Of your time.'

For someone who seemed to know pretty much what he was thinking for a good proportion of the time, Charlotte could be shockingly unperceptive sometimes. 'No. I think I've been demanding of *his* time, haven't I? It'll be my pleasure to pick him up from school on Wednesday.'

CHAPTER THIRTEEN

EDWARD WAS PLEASED to see that the school made him submit to a thorough check, to make sure he was who he said he was, before they would let him take Isaac. He'd been worried that Charlotte's husband might try something, and it seemed that his father had, too, because when Edward had broached the matter quietly with him he'd told him that was all seen to.

'So. What shall we do, then?'

The feeling that he was playing hookey was almost overwhelming. He wasn't, of course. The clinic knew exactly where he was, and he was just taking a few hours from the hundreds he was owed. But Edward didn't let that spoil the fantasy.

'What would *you* like to do?'

He dumped his keys and phone onto the hall table, and extricated Isaac from his backpack and coat.

'We could play a game on the internet. Or play football. Or perhaps you'd like to go to the park?'

Isaac nodded. He, too, had an air of being about to embark on an adventure. 'The park.'

'Okay. Do you think we should take some supplies with us? In case we get lost? You never know what might happen.'

Isaac smiled. 'Stay with me. I know my way around.'

'Okay. But perhaps we'll take some juice. And one of those fruit and nut bars your mum bought.'

'Mmm. Good idea.'

They rambled together through a small wooded area, picking up fallen branches to swish on the path in front of them. Edward turned over stones with his foot, and they both inspected the creatures which lived in the damp darkness below them.

'Look. A piece of flint.' He held out the broken pebble for Isaac to see.

'What's that?'

'Flint's a type of stone. A long time ago cavemen used to make axes and arrowheads out of flint. It's very hard.'

Isaac inspected the stone carefully. 'Can we make an axe out of this?'

'Maybe. It's a little small. Let's find a bigger

piece and perhaps we can take it home and give it a try.'

They searched together and found a bigger piece of flint. Edward put it into his pocket, and then saw a couple of flat, circular stones on the ground. 'Hey, look at these. Do you know how to skim stones?'

'No.'

Edward grinned. 'We'll collect some of these up, then, and I'll show you.'

The house was quiet when Charlotte got back home. The meeting with Edward's father had been longer than she'd thought it would be, and she was tired. She didn't much feel like cooking straight away, but she was going to have to.

'Hey? Guys...?' She called into the silence and only silence answered her. Perhaps they were out in the garden, playing football. She walked through to the kitchen and opened the back door.

No one there. Edward's car was parked in front of the house, and his suit jacket was slung over the bannisters. He must have walked down to the school.

Even if he had they should be back by now. He'd been due to collect Isaac more than two hours ago.

Charlotte pulled out her phone and checked it. No
calls or texts from the school. That meant that everything had gone to plan. Flipping through her
address book, she found the entry for Edward's
mobile and called it. Tapping her foot while the
call connected, she then let out a huff of exas-
peration when the tones of his mobile chimed out
from the hall table.

'Edward. Where *are* you?'

She wasn't sure whether to be cross or worried.
She dropped her bag onto the hall table, slung her
jacket over the bannister, and wandered into the
sitting room, sinking down onto the sofa.

'Where are *you*, Isaac?'

'Yeaaah!' Isaac jumped up and down, cheering.
'Six!'

Edward straightened, smiling with satisfaction.
'I think the smooth ones do better, don't you?'

Isaac nodded. 'Those big flat ones are the best,
though.'

'Hmm. Less air resistance. Larger surface area.'

Isaac nodded sagely, although it was doubtful
that he understood the finer points of it. Actually, for once, Edward wasn't much interested in
the finer points. Just in counting the number of

times their stones skipped across the water out loud with Isaac.

'I'm hungry.'

'Are you? We've had our drinks and...' Edward looked at his watch, his heart sinking when he saw the time. He felt in his pocket for his mobile and realised that he must have left it at home when he changed his jacket. 'Isaac, we've got to get going, mate. Your mum will be waiting for us.'

The list of possibilities was endless. A car accident. The lake. Surely Edward couldn't be so irresponsible as to take Isaac out on the lake—not after what had happened at the weekend. She couldn't think about that any more; it was making her feel sick. Peter's face flipped up into the void that not thinking about a freak accident had left. Could *he* have taken Isaac? Perhaps Edward was out looking for him?

She was being alarmist. They were probably out somewhere together. But Edward was normally so responsible. Charlotte couldn't imagine that he'd possibly become as involved with a game of football as he did on a day to day basis with his piles of papers and the intricate problems that his patients posed.

One of them had been taken ill. Perhaps she should call the local hospital. But wouldn't Edward have called? Left a message for her on his own home phone if he couldn't remember her mobile number? She checked the answering machine again. Nothing.

Where were they?

Edward had hoisted Isaac up on to his shoulders, was striding out as fast as he could without dislodging the boy from his perch. He should have left a note for Charlotte, telling her where they were. Or remembered to bring his mobile with him. That would have solved the problem. It was too late now. All he could do was hope that she wasn't worrying about Isaac.

He loped up the drive, gravel scrunching beneath his feet. There was no opportunity to pull his keys out of his pocket because the front door flew open. He could see from the way she rubbed her hand across her face that Charlotte was upset, but by the time he reached her she seemed to have regained some of her composure.

'Isaac! How was your day, sweetie?' Her eyes were red, but she was smiling, trying to pretend to Isaac that nothing was the matter. He let Isaac down and the boy ran to her to give her a hug.

'We had a brilliant time, Mum. We've been skimming stones. We've got a special method.'

Her gaze flipped up towards Edward at the mention of the special method and her lips pursed. Before he had a chance to apologise she was smiling at Isaac again.

'That's great. You're going to have to show me how you do that.'

'We've got a piece of flint, too.' Isaac twisted his face up towards Edward. 'Edward's going to make it into an axe.'

Right now, putting an axe anywhere within Charlotte's reach might not be such a good idea. She shot him another glare, and Edward put his hands into his pockets. He didn't particularly want to go into the house, or to be anywhere near her at the moment. Generally speaking, keeping out of the way until it all blew over was his preferred modus operandi in these situations.

'What's for tea, Mum?'

'Wait and see. Go inside, now, and take your coat off.' She stood aside as Isaac ran past her and into the house, then directed her gaze at Edward.

He already had his car keys in his hand, and

had pressed the remote to unlock the doors. She stood, arms folded, in the doorway. 'And where do you think you're going?'

Nowhere. Anywhere. 'I've…um…got to pick something up from the hospital.'

'Something important, no doubt?'

'I guess it must be.' He turned towards the car and heard the safety catch on the front door flip. Felt her hand catch in the crook of his arm, spinning him round.

'Afraid?'

'Yep. Terrified.'

He faced her at last. She was trembling with an emotion that he found hard to identify. A cocktail, maybe, of all the feelings that he didn't much want to think about at the moment.

'And running's the best option, is it?'

'I'd prefer to call it a tactical retreat.'

'Call it whatever you like.'

Her chin jutted provocatively. Eyes golden in the early evening sunshine. Her hair was slightly mussed, as if she had dragged it out of the neat knot that she usually wore it in for work and not bothered to comb it.

'Look. You're angry…' It was a very old cliché, but she was one of those people who became even more beautiful when angry. 'I'll let you go and see to Isaac...' He wanted to kiss her.

'Unless you hadn't noticed, Isaac's perfectly capable of switching the TV on by himself and sitting in front of it for ten minutes.' Perfectly on cue, the sound of a children's song washed through from the living room and Isaac's voice joined in with the melody.

'All the same...'

'Don't you dare...'

He felt her hand brush against his and the hairs on his arm stood on end. She pulled the car keys out of his hand and flipped the locking mechanism. Two beeps and a flash of the headlights told Edward that his car had just changed sides and was firmly in her camp now.

He didn't much blame it. She was difficult to resist. Throwing a backwards glance at the treacherous machine, he stalked into the house.

Isaac's head popped up over the back of the sofa. 'Edward. Come and see...'

All his resistance melted. That cornered feeling, which he usually dealt with stony-faced and emotionless, didn't matter any more. 'Hey, buddy.' He strode into the sitting room and plumped himself down next to the boy. 'Have you washed your hands?'

Isaac inspected his grubby fingers. 'No.'

'Well, you'd better do that. Mine could do with a wash as well.' He led Isaac into the kitchen, kicking the plastic box that he stood on to reach the counter-tops in front of the sink. He squirted a dollop of soap into Isaac's palm and then soaped his own fingers.

'Is Mum angry with us?' the boy whispered conspiratorially.

'Nah. Not with you.'

'You?'

'Don't you worry about that. I'll handle it.' Edward didn't bother with any details of exactly how, on the basis that he hadn't formulated them yet.

'Do you want to borrow my ray gun?' Isaac twisted round to face him, splashing water onto his shirt.

'Thanks. But I think I'll manage.' He bent down, keeping his voice low. 'We don't want to hurt her, do we?'

Isaac shook his head, taking the other end of the towel that Edward was drying his own hands with.

'I'll tell you what...' There were no signs of food

preparation in the kitchen. Charlotte had clearly been spending her time glued to the front window, waiting for him to bring Isaac home. 'Do you like Chinese food?'

Isaac nodded.

'Okay, then. I'll go out and get some.' Isaac shot him a questioning look. Clearly takeaways didn't figure much in his experience. 'I'll bring it home and we can eat it here.'

'You don't need to do that. I can have something ready in half an hour.'

Charlotte's voice sounded from the doorway. If she'd heard the bit about the ray gun she was clearly undaunted by it.

If she was so keen on him staying in, then she was going to have to put up with the consequences.

Edward reached for the takeaway menu, taped to the door of the fridge, and handed it to her. 'There's a nice place just around the corner. I'll phone in our order and go and pick it up. We can be eating in fifteen minutes.'

She gave a little huff and unfolded the card. The strains of another children's tune floated in from the sitting room and Isaac dropped his end of the towel and ran in to see what was happening on the television.

'Okay.' Edward closed the door into the sitting room behind the boy. 'You want to talk.'

She didn't really. But when Edward had started to retreat back into himself, his face losing all the animation that she saw whenever he talked with Isaac, she'd panicked. It had been as if she was losing him back into the realms of considered thought and few words.

She twisted her lips together, pretending to read the menu. He came closer.

'Afraid?' He plucked the menu from her hands and held it behind his back.

'Terrified.'

'Good.' That tantalising half-smile. 'I won't be needing the ray gun, then.'

'If you want to get a takeaway you'd better do it. Otherwise it'll be no quicker than if I cook.'

'If it's an apology you want…'

'No.' She'd overreacted. She was the one who ought to be apologising.

'I'm sorry. I should have let you know where we were. I lost track of time and you understandably got worried. It won't happen again.'

'It's okay. It doesn't matter.'

His blue eyes. You could always tell what was going on in Edward's head by those eyes. Now they were dark, as if an old anger had seized him.

'It does. I know that I can't really understand because I'm not a parent....'

'What?' Where had *that* come from?

'I'm not stupid. I know what people think of me.' He turned away from her, one hand slicking his hair back across his head. 'That I'm too bound up with my books to even notice what's going on under my nose.'

Not that again. 'Face me, Edward.'

'Is that better?' When he turned, his face was brooding, angry from the hurt that seemed to have steeped in his soul for a long time now.

'A little bit.'

This was like a crazy game. Each trying to drive the other away, protect themselves, and yet fascinated by each other.

Unable to resist the temptation to dig deeper. Charlotte stepped forward. 'Touch me.'

He looked at her as if she'd gone stark, staring mad. If she'd taken a moment to think about what she'd just said then she would have agreed with him completely.

'Like this?' His fingers trailed the line of her jaw. 'Or this?'

His other arm snaked around her waist in a strong, domineering motion and suddenly she was pressed against him. She should have known better than to taunt Edward.

Charlotte reached up, cradling his jaw in her hands. Not even the fact that Isaac was in the next room could stop her now. 'Now. Listen to me.'

'I'm listening.'

He was listening all right. She had every piece of his attention, from the strong curl of his body to the ever-fascinating eddies of his mind. It was all-encompassing, irresistible.

Charlotte took a deep breath. 'You should have let me know where you were, but I should have trusted that Isaac would be safe with you.'

'And...?'

His anger had subsided and she could feel the tautness of his frame relax against hers. Melting, almost...

'I just...'

'Find it hard to trust?'

Was she that transparent? 'Yes. I suppose I do. It's a big world out there, and Isaac's starting to be interested in it. My job is to keep him safe, make sure that he's got what he needs, and...'

'Let him go. Just a bit, maybe.'

'Yeah. Just a bit.' She reached up and touched the side of his face with her fingertips. 'Who says that you don't understand?'

He let her go abruptly. Probably just as well. Their bodies seemed to have taken on a life of their own. Moving against each other with an almost imperceptible but blissful friction.

He shook his head as if to clear it. 'It's not rocket science. You've had to fend for yourself and Isaac for a long time, now. Isaac's father, the one person who should be helping you, is only making things worse. You've had to struggle to make ends meet, and been chased out of your home by debt collectors. I would think that trust issues go hand in hand with that.'

'Hmm. Life's a bit more complicated than rocket science sometimes.'

Edward leaned back against the kitchen counter, his hungry eyes still on her. 'Rocket science isn't really that complicated. One of those illustrations that doesn't stand up to too much scrutiny.'

For a moment Charlotte could see the lure of his books. Something that was constant in an ever-changing world. If she could have seen the same beauty in numbers and science that Edward did...

Damn the books. They couldn't give him this.

She stepped forward and found him there, ready. His body seemed to mould to hers—a close fit that left no room for anything else to come between them.

She kissed him. She couldn't help it. And once she'd brushed her lips against his she couldn't help but go back for more. His response was thrilling, strong and tender all at the same time.

One hand travelled lightly down her back. Across the rise of her hips and to the top of her leg. This was too much. She'd bitten off far more than she could chew.

'Isaac...' She just managed to get the word out.

'Yeah...'

His grip on her loosened, but Charlotte couldn't bring herself to pull away.

'He's just in the next room.'

She wasn't telling him, she was telling herself. Giving herself the one and only reason that could stop her from keeping going until all the pent-up frustration came screaming from her lungs.

'We should stop.'

Edward seemed as disinclined to bring this to

a close as she was, but he was the stronger. He gave her one last, head-spinning kiss before he gripped her shoulders, carefully propelling her backwards, away from him.

'That's...sensible.' Her cheeks were burning, and she still couldn't quite catch her breath.

'Yes. I'd better go and get us something to eat. Before...'

'Before we get too hungry...'

'Yes.' He pulled the takeaway menu out of his back pocket. 'What would you like?'

'Anything. Surprise me.'

His lips twitched into a half-grin before he straightened his face. 'All right. I'll be fifteen minutes.'

Enough time to splash cold water on her face and take a breath. 'Have you got chopsticks here?'

'No, I'll get some.'

He opened the kitchen door and disappeared into the living room. Charlotte heard him exchange a few words with Isaac, and as the front door slammed she shook her head. It was going to take a lot longer than fifteen minutes to get Edward out of her system.

CHAPTER FOURTEEN

'IS IT SO very wrong to feel like celebrating?'
Charlotte wondered if she sounded cold-hearted.

'No.' Paula swirled her herbal tea thoughtfully
in her cup. 'It's exactly the right thing to do.
You've got to look forward, not back.'

Paula clearly thought that Charlotte was being
brave about this. It was nothing of the sort. Ever
since she'd received the Decree Absolute this
morning Charlotte had wanted to do nothing but
dance. And, finding herself alone with Paula in
the employees' lounge, she'd been unable to con-
tain her news.

'Actually, it's quite a relief. I was afraid my husband…' Charlotte couldn't help smiling '…my
ex-husband would make some kind of objection
somewhere along the line.'

'From what you've said in the past…' Paula
looked at Charlotte thoughtfully. 'Okay, so you've
asked for no maintenance. Your ex didn't ask for

any rights to visit Isaac. Am I right in thinking that this guy was bad news?'

'Between you and me…?'

Paula nodded. 'Of course.' Paula might gossip, along with the rest of them, but she knew how to keep a confidence.

'Yeah. Very bad news. He hasn't seen Isaac for months, even though I've asked him time and time again if he'd come.'

Paula snorted in disgust. 'What kind of slug doesn't want to see a cute little guy like Isaac? No wonder you want to celebrate. You want to come down to Drake's tonight? We could crack open a bottle of champagne.'

'I'd love to. But I've got to go and pick that cute little guy up.'

Paula nodded. 'And the cute big one?'

'There's only one guy in my life who's even re-motely cute. And he's three feet tall…' Charlotte told herself that you couldn't really call Edward cute.

'Yeah, right. You're either blind, or crazy, or…' Paula grinned, her words taking on a sing-song intonation '…you're telling porkies.'

'I'm just out of one bad relationship. I think I'll

take some time to pause for a breath.' Charlotte shrugged. 'Twenty years or so.'

Paula leaned towards her. 'I wouldn't leave it twenty seconds if I could get my hands on Edward North.'

'Who says I can?'

Only about half the clinic. And the other half reckoned she already had. Keeping secrets about what you did out of hours was easy enough. Keeping secrets about how you felt about the people you worked with was nigh on impossible in such a small community.

Paula had the grace not to remind her of the gossip. 'Whatever. But in another four hours' time it's going to be the weekend. Tell me you'll find *something* to do to celebrate, eh?'

'Yes, I will.'

Paula nodded. 'Life's too short to worry about what other people say. Even me.'

'Thanks, Paula.' Charlotte looked at her watch. 'I've got to go. I've a clinic in twenty minutes.'

'Edward North?'

'Yes, Edward North—if you must know.'

'Two more to go?' They were in one of the Hunter Clinic's plush consulting rooms.

'Yes.' Charlotte flipped through the notes. 'April Ashe is next. She's just coming in for a follow-up visit.'

'Ah, yes, April. Have you seen her yet?'

'Yes, she's in the waiting area.'

'How is she?'

Charlotte laughed. 'Isn't that what she's here for? For *you* to say how she is?'

'You know what I mean.'

Yes, she did. And it was a question that Edward wouldn't have asked just a couple of weeks ago. 'She looks great. She's got a new dress on.'

Edward searched her face for some clue. 'How would you know that? Or am I intruding into a knowledge base that's for you to know and the male of the species to wonder about.'

'You'll have to wonder.' Charlotte grinned at him. It was simple, really. When Charlotte had admired April's yellow and white summer dress her mother had said it was new. But it was good to keep Edward wondering from time to time.

This time April walked into the consulting room alone. 'Hi, April.' Edward got to his feet. 'You look very nice today.'

April nodded. 'Thanks.'

Charlotte wondered whether he would ask, but

he didn't. Instead he set to, examining the skin on the side of April's face. 'That's healing very nicely, April. What do you think of it?'

'It's…different. Good… It itches a bit still.'

'Yes, that's natural. It itches as it heals.' Edward smiled. 'You've been massaging the oil that Charlotte gave you into it? And I can see you've been keeping out of the sun.'

'Yes.'

'Good.' Edward returned to his chair. 'Well, I don't think that I need to see you again.' He smiled at April and she grinned back.

Experience had taught Charlotte that this was the point where she stepped in.

'You will, of course, be seeing Charlotte again, and she'll monitor your progress. But I was wondering whether you had any questions for me.'

Okay. This was new. Usually he left the questions part to the nurses.

'Um… Not really…'

'Hmm. So what's this question you don't *really* need to ask, then?'

April smiled self-consciously at him. 'Well, I'm going to my end-of-year party at school in a couple of weeks' time.'

'Ah. That might be a little out of my area of expertise.'

He looked at Charlotte and she raised her eyebrows at him. So he was going to leave her something to do, at least.

'I think that April would be interested in knowing whether another couple of weeks is going to make an appreciable difference to the look of the scar. And whether she can use a little make-up. Is that right?'

April nodded. 'Yeah. There's someone I...'

'Yes. Of course. Well, the wound's been dry for a while now, and there's no reason why you shouldn't start to use light cosmetics occasionally, as long as they don't irritate your skin. Charlotte can advise on which types to use and so on. As to the look of it...' He paused, thinking for a while. 'Generally speaking, I'd expect that area to look better in two or three weeks' time than it does now. May I ask you a question, April?'

'Sure. What is it?'

'Well, it's a long time since I was your age...' He paused, as if waiting for a contradiction.

'Mmm,' April agreed.

'But I can certainly remember it.' He shot a stern look at Charlotte, who was barely repressing her laughter. 'And I have to say that any young man who disregards your smile and your personality, and who only sees a scar, isn't worth your time.'

'That's what my mother says...' April gave him a wry look.

'Well, it must be right, then.' Edward snapped his notepad shut with an air of finality.

'But...' April looked at him thoughtfully. 'But when I said I wanted my scar done she was all for it. So was my dad.'

Some of Isaac's questions prompted that very same baffled look from Edward, but he regrouped almost instantly. 'I look at it like this. What I do can't change who you are, because you're already special. My aim is to give you what you deserve.'

A slow smile spread across April's face. 'Nice one. Thanks.'

'You're very welcome, April.' Edward rose from his seat. 'Well, I can see that you ladies have some...um...things to talk about. Is your mother outside? I'd just like to have a quick word with her.'

April nodded and watched him go, before turning to Charlotte. 'You know, I thought that Dr

North was a bit stand-offish. But he's really nice, isn't he?'

Charlotte laughed. 'Yes, he is. Really nice.'

Charlotte wished Paula a good weekend and watched her go through the doors to the outside lobby. She waited for a few minutes and then made for Edward's office. She'd been saving her good news until they could talk uninterrupted.

'You got it, then?' He looked up when she tapped on the door, pushing the papers in front of him aside.

'How did you know?'

'I saw the courier delivery for you on the reception desk this morning.'

'Okay.' Charlotte sat down. 'So I had a delivery. It could have been anything.'

'That's just the first of my observations. The second was that the envelope was my father's stationery.'

'So you went to the Sherlock Holmes School of Medicine, did you? You'll have to do better than that. It could have been a letter from him telling me that there was some kind of problem.'

'Ah. Yes, it could.' Edward leaned back in his chair, the tips of his fingers touching to form an inverted V. 'But then you wouldn't have been looking like a cat that's just got the cream all afternoon.'

'I haven't!' That Edward had noticed the letter and known where it was from was hardly surprising. That he'd noticed *her* was still a new enough experience to make her shiver with pleasure.

'Yes, you have.' Edward gathered up some papers and stuffed them into his briefcase. 'Let's go.'

He picked up the heaviest of her shopping bags and ushered her out of his office.

He nodded a goodnight to Ethan Hunter, who had appeared from the lobby, and kept walking when Ethan spoke.

'Do you have a moment, Charlotte?'

'Yes, of course.'

It was all very well for Edward to walk on ahead, as if they both just happened to be leaving work at the same time, rather than together. But the canvas shopping bag with 'Smart Girls Recycle' emblazoned across it was hardly going to be his.

'Mrs Ashe asked to speak with me before she left.'

'Is there a problem?' Charlotte had thought that

the session with April had gone well, but generally clients stopped to complain, rather than praise.

'She was very pleased with the way that April's procedure has been handled, and she especially mentioned how well you'd looked after her. I hear you even gave her some make-up advice. Well done.'

'Oh! Thank you, Ethan.' Perhaps it was relief, but she thought she saw a flicker of warmth in Ethan's normally impassive face. 'It was very nice of Mrs Ashe to take the time to speak with you.'

'She mentioned that Edward was very kind, as well...' Ethan was clearly a little perplexed by the concept.

'He always does his best for every patient.' Now probably wasn't the time to go into any apparent change in Edward's demeanour.

Ethan nodded. 'Yes, of course. And it's always good to hear that our clients value our people as much as we do. Passing their praise on is one of the more pleasant duties which falls to me when Leo's not around.'

'I appreciate it that you did. It means a lot.' Charlotte smiled up at Ethan and made a move towards the exit.

Ethan walked with her. 'You have a son?'

He'd clearly decided that this was one of those getting-to-know-you moments that a good employer should take with his employees. Charlotte wished he'd chosen a time when Edward hadn't been waiting for her outside.

'Yes. Isaac's five.'

'Must be quite a handful, then. Was he the boy I saw Edward playing with in his office a couple of weeks ago?'

'Um… Yes.'

'I've never seen Edward look so animated.' Ethan was smiling now. A little distant, as if he was thinking about something else at the same time, but definitely a smile. 'You and Edward make a good team.'

Charlotte swallowed hard and decided to interpret *good team* in a purely professional context. 'Isaac has a way of involving people. I suppose all children do…'

'Yeah. I guess they do. But Edward's a pretty tough nut to crack.' The smile faded and was replaced by Ethan's usual thoughtful look. The one that implied his thoughts on the matter were not particularly happy ones.

'No one's that tough.'

Ethan raised one eyebrow. 'I wouldn't go as far

as to say that.' He stepped forward, opening the door to the lobby for her, and Charlotte walked through.

Edward was waiting there, her shopping bag nestled against his own briefcase at his feet. He nodded briskly at Ethan, who returned the nod and disappeared along the hallway.

'Everything okay?' Edward waited until Ethan was out of earshot.

'Yeah, fine. Mrs Ashe told Ethan that you and I had done a good job with April, and he stopped to say thank you.'

'That's nice.'

'He said we made a good team.'

'Well, we do, don't we?'

That slight quirk of Edward's lips told her that he, at least, didn't have his mind completely on the professional. 'Why are you looking so glum? You've just had a vote of thanks from the boss. Ethan doesn't say these things unless he means them.'

What Ethan had really meant was beyond Charlotte. He'd seemed genuinely pleased for the little family unit which was forming before his eyes, but somehow… Charlotte sighed. If Ethan thought that it was beyond his own reach, then Charlotte was inclined to think it was beyond hers, too.

'What? What's the matter?'

'Nothing. Let's go home.'

She'd pushed the boat out and bought steak for dinner, cooking it in a peppered sauce with home-made chips. Edward and Isaac had tucked in with an almost identical glee, and been unanimous in their praise.

'I've been thinking.' Edward was helping her stack the dishwasher while Isaac played in the garden.

'Oh-oh. That generally means trouble...' She smiled at him.

He shot her a look of amused reproach. 'Would you like to go out tomorrow evening? To celebrate...or perhaps to commiserate. Whatever you feel like doing, I'll keep you company.'

'I feel like... No. Let's not do anything, eh? My marriage is over now, and I don't want to look back. I want to look forward.'

'Fair enough. So why don't you just let me treat you, then? My mother's coming over tomorrow afternoon, and she can look after Isaac for the evening if you'd like. We can go somewhere nice.'

Going out. On a Saturday night. It was years since she'd had the money to go anywhere, nice or otherwise, let alone pay for babysitters and...
'I don't really have anything to wear...'

He shrugged. 'You have clothes. We'll go somewhere where clothes are *de rigueur*.'

She couldn't help but laugh. 'Okay. Thank you. I'd love to.'

His smirk looked far too much as if this had been a plan and not an off-the-cuff invitation. 'Good. Mum'll be here about three tomorrow.'

It all seemed to go like clockwork. Edward's mother arrived on the doorstep at five to three the following day, and burst into the house like a friendly tornado. She kissed Edward, hugged Charlotte as if she'd know her for years, and made a beeline for Isaac, who was sitting on the floor playing with a construction set.

'That looks interesting.' Penny North had sat down on the sofa and was now looking hard at Isaac's handiwork.

'It's a spaceship.' Isaac looked up at her.

'Well, of course it is. Silly me.'

Isaac made his decision and opted to trust this

stranger with some more information. 'Look, this is the engine.'

'Oh, I see. How clever.'

Edward nudged Charlotte. 'You want to leave them to it?'

His breath caressed her neck and she shivered. Suddenly it all seemed real. She had a date for tonight. Not just any old date, but a darkly handsome, sophisticated, talk-all-night date. And it looked as if Isaac was making his own arrangements for the evening.

'Yes. Let's go and make a cup of tea.'

After Kathy, his mother had seemed to give up all hope of seeing a woman, let alone a child, in Edward's house. Charlotte had gone upstairs to change and he sat with his mother on the patio, watching while Isaac ran around the garden. He liked this more than he was prepared to admit. His mother was clearly overjoyed, and had exceeded all expectations in her enthusiasm for both Charlotte and Isaac.

'Can't you take her somewhere nicer than that, Edward?'

'I like it there.'

'Yes, but a girl wants to be taken somewhere

glamorous.' His mother waved her hand, encom-
passing all the glitzy nightspots that London had
to offer. 'Somewhere she can kick her heels up
and forget about everything.'

'Like Dad did with you?'

'Yes, now you mention it. Your father wined
and dined me until I was far too giddy to say no
when he asked me to marry him.'

'Don't jump the gun, Mother. We're just friends.'

'Yes, and that's all you'll ever be if you carry on
like this. Just call upstairs, tell her to put her best
dress on, and get on the phone and book somewhere nice....'

'She doesn't have a best dress. She's been living
hand to mouth for the last few years...'

His mother let out a tut of disapproval. 'Well,
couldn't you have taken her out and bought her
something?'

'I could have tried, but she wouldn't have let me.
She's...proud.' *Proud* wasn't really the word for
it. Charlotte didn't have a lot of trust. But Edward
didn't want to go there with his mother. 'And she
looks great anyway, with or without a new dress.'

His mother nodded in satisfaction at the asser-
tion. 'Well...yes, all right, then. I can see the difficulty. But for goodness' sakes tell her how nice

she looks, won't you? You can't expect women to just know what you're thinking.'

That was the thing. He'd thought that Kathy had known what he was thinking—if anyone should have done it would have been her. And she'd said he had no emotional commitment. Those words had been seared into his brain and had stayed there, like the ultimate condemnation.

'I don't expect anyone to know what I'm thinking.'

His mother quirked a smile. 'Well, that's just as well, dear. You'd already lost me by the time you were about ten. But this is different. We're not talking about advanced mathematics. We're talking about...' His mother groped for the right word.

'Emotions?'

'Yes, exactly. We all have the same emotions, irrespective of whether we can do complex equations in our heads.'

That was a matter of opinion. But Edward was saved from the rigours of that particular debate by Isaac, who tripped over his own feet and suddenly toppled, flat on his face, onto the grass. In a movement that was rapidly becoming instinctive Edward rose and hurried towards the boy.

'Hey, there.' Edward inspected him rapidly for any damage. 'Okay, mate. You're all right.'

Isaac didn't seem to think so, and clung to him, crying. Edward gave him a hug and his sobs subsided. 'There you are. Just a bit of a shock, eh? Have you hurt yourself?'

'No.' Isaac seemed ready to start careening around the lawn again, but then his attention was drawn to the patio.

Charlotte was wearing a simple white dress, with a lacy bodice that showed the curve of her shoulders and upper arms. Her light brown hair tumbled around her shoulders, shining in the sun. He wasn't close enough to see her eyes, but Edward knew that they would be shining, too.

'What do you think, mate? Doesn't your mother look gorgeous?'

Isaac nodded and Edward let him go. The boy rushed towards her, shouting at the top of his voice.

'Muuuum! Edward says you look gorgeous.'

Well, that was one way of doing it. His mother obviously approved, and Charlotte went pink with pleasure. He almost didn't dare go any closer, in case she captured him in some kind of spell.

'Well, thank you.' She was holding both of

Isaac's hands, trying to keep them away from her dress. 'I'll just go and clean him up…'

'That's fine.' Edward hoisted the boy upwards, tucking him under his arm, and Isaac squealed with delight. 'We don't want to get your mother all dirty, do we?'

Finally they were alone. Instructions had been given, telephone numbers written down, and Charlotte had elicited a promise from Isaac to be extra good for the whole of the evening. The taxi had arrived, and she had allowed Edward to help her into it.

'This is nice.'

She seemed excited, even though she didn't yet know where they were going. Edward wondered whether it would be appropriate to put his arm along the back of the seat, and decided that he should probably wait until the way home.

'I didn't want to worry about parking. Or having a glass of wine if I felt like it.'

She nodded and smiled at him. That warm, bubbly smile of hers which so lifted his spirits when he saw it at work. Here, combined with the fact that she smelled absolutely wonderful, and with her skin just inches away from his touch…Edward was lost

CHAPTER FIFTEEN

THE TAXI LET them off in Soho. Bubbling with life, on a warm summer's evening, the atmosphere was going to Charlotte's head. Edward took her hand, easing them through the crowded pavements.

'Where are we going?'

'Here.' He stopped suddenly, then descended a set of steps which seemed to run down to a basement. Opening the door at the bottom, he gave his name to a woman, handed his jacket over, and they were waved through.

She already knew what this place was. Soft jazz was floating towards them, beckoning them into a small auditorium. They were shown to a table and the waiter gave them each a menu, and left.

The place wasn't posh, or glitzy, nor was it sleazy. It was the kind of place that no one other than a real jazz enthusiast would know about, and its clientele didn't come here to be seen, but to listen.

'Is this okay?' He leaned across the table, his

mouth almost touching her cheek. 'We can go somewhere else if you don't like it.'

'It's wonderful. Can we stay?'

He nodded in satisfaction. 'Of course. What would you like to drink?'

The long cushioned seats were comfortable, and the wine that the waiter brought to the table was excellent, but it was really all about the music. A three-piece band played smooth, moody melodies, which made everything seem so very easy. She slid along the seat, closer to Edward, so that they could exchange a few words without distracting anyone.

The band finished their set to enthusiastic applause and a great deal of crashing about as they left the small stage.

'Would you like something to eat? We've got about half an hour before they bring the next band on.'

The waiters suddenly seemed to leap into action as they were beckoned by one table or another.

'There's going to be another one?'

'More than one. Until about four in the morning, usually.' Edward grinned at her.

'And how many times have you stayed until then?'

'Once or twice. I used to come here a lot, but not so much lately.'

'Can't do the late nights, eh?'

He shrugged. 'Not really. But you can come in here, have a glass of wine, go home early and be tucked up in bed by ten. It's more a state of mind.'

He did seem younger here. As if his quiet manner was more a result of relaxation than introspection. 'Are we going to stay for the next set?'

He nodded. 'As long as you like. The plan doesn't go any further than this.'

'What plan's that?'

'The plan for the evening. It ends here. We're on our own now.'

They weren't, of course. Charlotte knew that they had to get back at a respectable time so that Penny could get on home. But for a few sweet hours it seemed as if there was nothing else in the world. At some point Edward's arm seemed to have snaked along the cushions behind her. She appeared to have moved a little closer to him, and now she was in the circle of his warmth, talking to him, listening to the music with him.

The spell hardly broke when they left the club. The streets were dark now, lit by the glittering lights of Chinatown, and they strolled together through the crowds until they reached Oxford Street, where Edward flagged down a taxi.

The roads were clear of the daytime traffic, and it was starting to rain. Yellow light streaked the windows of the cab as they reached the leafy suburb of Hampstead. A sudden left turn, which would have thrown her against Edward if she hadn't already been leaning against him, and they were home.

'He's fast asleep.' Penny was smiling and seemed in a hurry to be off. 'I gave him some tea and he ran around in the garden until he dropped. Then we watched some TV together and he was out like a light when I put him to bed.'

Charlotte could hardly get a thank-you out before Edward had kissed his mother and was walking her to her car. He watched her out of the drive and then turned back to the house.

It was suddenly very quiet. And Edward was abruptly the only focus of her attention.

'Would you...um...like a cup of tea?'

'No.' He moved a little closer. 'Would you?'

'No. Not really.'

She knew what was coming next. It was drawing her in, like the dark, unknown depths of his eyes, with a force that she couldn't resist. Didn't want to resist. However unsure she was, however hard it was to trust Edward, tonight she didn't seem to recognise any of that. All she saw was him.

'I'll…I'll just go and check on Isaac.' Maybe he was awake. Maybe that would solve the debate that was going on in the back of her mind about what to do next.

'Okay.' He backed off, and flopped down onto the sofa.

Isaac was sleeping soundly, Stinky clutched in his arms, and Charlotte walked slowly back downstairs. That was it, then. It was just her and Edward.

'Is he okay?'

His voice was low, like honey on her senses.

'Yes, he's fast asleep.'

'Just you and me, then.' He motioned her to come and sit down next to him.

'Yes. Just the two of us.' She perched herself on the edge of the sofa, her legs tucked under her. For a moment it seemed that they would simply sit like this for a few minutes and then say goodnight.

Then he reached forward, curling his arms

around her waist, almost lifting her onto his lap. His movements were so slow, so deliberate, that they might be mistaken for hesitancy, but there was no uncertainty about him. It was just Edward, doing what he did best, squeezing every last drop from each moment that passed.

'I had a great evening.' She leaned towards him, speaking quietly into his ear.

'Had?'

'Am having. Are you being pedantic?'

'No. Just working out where I stand.'

'This is where you stand.' She kissed his jaw.

He said nothing. For a moment she thought that she'd done the wrong thing, that this wasn't what he wanted. Then he turned and kissed her. Long and deep, leaving her breathless and melting in his arms.

'I've been wanting to do that all evening.' One hand rested lightly on her leg, travelling upwards towards her thigh.

'I've been wanting you to…' He didn't let her finish, before he kissed her again. That was okay. She'd said all she needed to, and now all she wanted was to be part of the strong, flowing tide of his passion.

'Come upstairs.'

'We'll have to be quiet. Isaac...'

'That's okay. We won't disturb him.' He kissed her again, his lips so soft on hers. So demanding. 'I'll stop if you get too *fortissimo*.'

'Funny man. What happens if *you* get too loud?'

'You'll just have to crack me over the head with a table lamp. Or suffocate me with a pillow. Plenty of options...'

A whole world of options, if those still waters ran as deep as she thought they might. More options than Charlotte really know how to deal with right now. But even that couldn't stop her.

'I'll bear it in mind.'

He smiled, that quiet half-smile which seemed touched with every possibility that she could think of, along with a few that she didn't know how to imagine. Then he gathered her close in his arms, lifting her effortlessly and making for the stairs.

Even though she'd been living here for two weeks now, Charlotte had never been inside his bedroom. She'd glimpsed pale, creamy walls bathed in sunlight when she passed by in the mornings, but had never dared to even put her head around the door. The first thing she noticed when he flipped on the lights was that, unlike pretty much every other room in the house, there were no books. Built-in wardrobes ran the full length of one wall, and a wide bed stood opposite the window, ready to catch the morning sun. It was like a soothing blank canvas for the rich pattern of Edward's thoughts.

He set her down onto her feet and closed the door quietly. Then he kissed her, backing her slowly towards the bed. 'Do you have…?'

'Yes.' He moved away for a moment, flipping open a drawer and taking out a box of condoms, putting it onto the small table by the bed.

'Thank you.' He made everything easy. Thought of the things she needed as well as the ones she wanted.

He reached around her, undoing the buttons which ran down the back of her dress. He slipped it from her shoulders, kissing each inch of flesh as he uncovered it. The fabric fell to her feet and she stepped out of it, kicking her sandals off.

'Say something, Edward.' She suddenly felt small and fearful in the shadow of his bulk.

'What can I say? You're beautiful beyond words.' He ran his fingertips down her arms. 'I want you more than I know how to express.'

'That's…' she gulped '…that's just fine.'

'Good.' His fingers again, tender on the side of her face. 'Because you put me at a loss, Charlotte.'

'That's just where we're supposed to be. If we weren't, then we wouldn't need each other to find the way.' She reached up to unbutton his shirt, pulling it open and off his shoulders.

She guessed she had his swimming to thank for the hard, muscular physique that was so good to look at, so warm and enticing when she ran her fingers across his chest. Each time he kissed her it was hotter. Deeper. Each time he laid his hand on her it was a little more demanding.

Before they even got to the bed they were both naked, trembling. He sat down on it, pulling her down onto his lap, astride him.

'Here.' He reached for the condoms, handing her one.

Slowly she rolled it down, loving the way that he gasped when her fingers touched him. Loving the warm feel of his skin when he pulled her close, lifting her. And then it went past loving, or adoring, or any of the other words that had seemed like something to aim for. Pure feeling washed over her when he lowered her slowly down, sliding inside her as he did so.

'Edward…' His name was the only thing on her mind.

'Charlotte…' He choked her name out, his hands twisting her hips so that they both gasped.

His hands, his mouth, caressed her. It was beyond bearing. Her body knew what to do, but he was holding her firmly in his lap, not letting her move the way she wanted to.

'Edward…please.'

One hand slipped between her legs and she almost cried out. He was intent on wringing every drop of pleasure from each moment, and the only doubt in Charlotte's mind was whether she was going to be able to bear it.

'I…can't…take much more of this.'

'Really?' His hand moved to her breast.

'Really. Edward…'

He didn't reply. He rolled his body round, until he was pinning her down on the bed, and with a look of unutterable tenderness slid inside her again. She felt her body mould to his, her hands grabbing at the sheets. Was that a moan? She put her hand to her mouth, biting hard on her knuckle.

He twisted his hips and her head spun. He caressed her, capturing her gasps in a kiss, and she was his. No thought, no fear, just feeling flowing through her, washing her clean of everything other than him. She gazed into his eyes, because they were the only things that made sense any more, and saw them darken. Felt his body stiffen and knew that he, too, had finally reached the point where he was as lost as she was.

Suddenly he was all fire. Coaxing her on, raising the temperature to boiling point. Stronger, sweeter, until her body arched of its own accord and waves of pure feeling washed through her.

Edward couldn't trust himself to speak. If he did he would say he loved her, that he would do anything for her if she'd just stay with him. And that was surely just the heat of the moment.

He felt a cool trickle of sweat trace its way down his spine, pooling in the small of his back. She was so beautiful. So giving. Her body was still quivering, little jolts still shaking her after the one great explosion of feeling. Then, as he watched her face, seeming to find endless fascination in the ever-changing detail, she broke him completely. A single tear trickled from her eye.

'Okay, sweetheart?' Perhaps he had been too demanding. He hadn't been able to help himself.

She gave him a slow, lazy smile which said that

everything was better than okay. 'Yeah. Just fine. Happy tears.'

Charlotte wound her arms around his neck, pulling him close, and he rolled over onto his side, curling his body around hers. Perfectly happy. Perfectly... Just perfect, really.

They woke in the night and made love again, but when he opened his eyes in the morning she wasn't there. He hadn't really expected her to be. Isaac couldn't know about this just yet. Maybe one day—if they lasted that long.

He showered alone, and dressed, drawn downstairs by the sound of her voice and Isaac's. She looked up as he stood in the doorway of the kitchen and smiled.

'Good morning.'

'Yes, it *is* a good morning.' His whole body felt as if it had been bathed in sunshine.

She flushed a little. 'Did we wake you?'

He shook his head. Isaac raced out of the kitchen, ready to attack the day, and Edward took his place at the table.

'I was going to bring you breakfast in bed as soon as I'd finished with Isaac.' Her mouth twisted in an expression of regret.

'Just as well you didn't.' He pulled her onto his

lap and kissed her on the cheek. 'If I'd woken up and found you there I wouldn't have let you go.'

'No? Even if I'd had fresh coffee?'

He weighed the question up. 'Maybe if you'd had coffee... Is there any?'

'Right here.' She went to stand up, but he pulled her back down again.

'Charlotte, I know we have to keep this away from Isaac...'

'Yeah. I'm sorry. I just don't want to confuse him...'

'Don't be. I understand.' It didn't mean that he liked it, but he wouldn't hurt Isaac for anything. 'But that doesn't mean I won't be waiting for you. Tonight.'

She gave him a smile. 'Tonight it is, then. In the meantime, do you want some coffee?'

CHAPTER SIXTEEN

EDWARD WAS SMILING to himself. He could see
Charlotte from his office, passing and re-passing
the nurses' station. Something about the way she
moved sent memories of last night and the night
before pulsing down his spine.

He shouldn't be doing this. There were things to
do—cases to review, patients to see. Admittedly
there wasn't actually anything to do at this moment, but he was slipping. He hadn't touched the
paper he was writing for a week, nor had he been
swimming. He badly needed some thinking time.

The phone rang and Edward glared at it. He was
far too busy interrupting himself at the moment
to encourage anyone else to do so. He snatched
up the receiver.

'North.'

*'Edward, it's Ethan. I've a case here that I think
you might be interested in.'*

Something tingled at the back of his neck. The
excitement of a challenge. He could do with that

at the moment—before the tilt in the balance of his life became a catastrophic slide.

'I'll be right there.'

Edward was, indeed, interested. The surgery was slated for a couple of months hence, and it would be complicated, demanding, and require painstaking preparation. It was just the thing.

Their review of the notes was interrupted by the phone. Ethan's brow darkened. His habitual cool courtesy when dealing with the clinic staff was clearly being tested.

'Can you take a message please? I've asked for all of my calls to be put on hold for the next half-hour....' Someone spoke urgently at the other end of the line. 'Ah, Helen, it's you...' He listened again, and then nodded briskly. 'Okay. Yes, thanks, Helen. You were right to let me know. Put her through, please.'

Edward made to leave, but Ethan waved him back into his seat. 'I have to take this, but I won't be long.' He turned back to the phone. 'Olivia...?'

A pulse was beating at the side of Ethan's brow, but his face was fixed, impassive. The look of a soldier about to go into battle. He listened, concentrating on the phone and the notes that he was scribbling. 'Repeat that, please... Okay, got it. All

right, consider it done. We'll courier all the paperwork out to you.'

He placed the phone back gently into its cradle. Ethan seemed deep in thought and Edward
didn't ask.

'Can you do something for me?' Finally Ethan
spoke.

'Of course.'

'That was Olivia Fairchild. Leo's away, and
there are some problems with a visa for one of the
kids she's sending to the clinic. I'm not sure quite
what's involved, but I think there's just a declara-
tion of some sort to be made from our end. Olivia
will be travelling with the girl and her mother, so
we can send any necessary paperwork straight
through to her.'

Edward nodded. 'Leave it with me.' Was that
relief he saw on Ethan's face? It probably wasn't
anything to do with the legal complexities involved, because there weren't any. 'Give me your
notes.'

'Thanks.' Ethan made a few more jottings on
the pad in front of him and handed the paper over
to Edward. 'Appreciate it.'

It was like leading a double life. A triple life,
actually. There was the persona that she adopted

at work—the one that hardly noticed Edward was even there unless he was giving instructions of a medical nature. The one that she had fallen into at home, being a part of the unlikely family that she, Edward and Isaac seemed to have made for themselves. And there was the one which lasted from the time that Isaac went to bed through to the early hours of the morning.

Evenings spent by the piano, talking together or just keeping each other company. Or reading together, their limbs entwined, Charlotte with her book and Edward with his. Early nights, when they had the opportunity to do all the things that they dared not talk about during the day, and which were increasingly bleeding into her thoughts at the most inappropriate times.

'Where's Edward?'

She and Isaac were having tea in the kitchen together. Edward had made it back home only just in time to say goodnight to Isaac for the last three evenings, and Isaac had missed playing with him after tea.

'He's at the hospital, sweetie. He's got to stay and make sure that the people he's looking after are okay.'

Isaac frowned. 'What people?'

Good question. But her own uncertainties weren't the issue here. It had been less than two weeks since she and Edward had first spent the night together, and it had taken only a week before the slow, subtle sense that he was withdrawing from her became apparent. When he was there he was still as committed, still as quietly loving. He just wasn't there as much as he used to be.

'People who are sick, sweetie.' She leaned across the table towards Isaac. 'There's a little boy, about your age, who's had an accident and lost his thumb. Edward's going to give him a new one.'

Isaac regarded his own thumb thoughtfully. 'A bionic thumb...?'

'No, a real one.' Charlotte decided to skip the bit about how the child had lost two other fingers as well, and that the reconstruction of one side of his hand was ground-breaking in its complexity.

'Is that what Edward's doing now?'

Difficult to say. She'd heard about this particular case from one of the other doctors, not Edward. 'The operation's tomorrow. I expect he's preparing for it.'

'And Edward will make the boy better?'

'Yes, he will, sweetie.' Charlotte could give that assurance, at least, with a clear conscience.

'Good.'

Isaac seemed satisfied, even if Charlotte didn't share his confidence. Isaac was too young to remember the excuses that his father had made for being out every evening. Things to do at work. Client entertaining. She reminded herself that Edward was doing something worthwhile, and not running up debts that he couldn't pay.

She heard a noise at the front door and Isaac slipped down from his seat, running into the hallway. So different from the child who, just four weeks ago, had nearly jumped out of his skin when someone knocked on the door.

'Hey, buddy.'

She heard Edward's voice and suddenly all of her fears and uncertainties seemed unreasonable. Not that they stopped pinching at her heart, but for the time being they receded to mere what-ifs instead of painful certainty.

'Is he better?' Isaac was perched against Edward's side, tugging at his shoulder to gain his attention.

'Is who better?'

'That boy...?'

Edward's querying gaze lit on Charlotte's face.
'Isaac was asking where you were.' Charlotte
hadn't dared ask, thinking that it was assuming
a bit too much. 'I told him that you were making
another little boy well. The one you're operating
on tomorrow.'

'Ah.' He turned to Isaac. 'The boy's not better
yet, but he will be. We're taking good care of him,
and he's going to be just fine.' He set Isaac back
onto his feet and sat down.

'Would you like something to eat?'

He looked up at her. That dark blue gaze made
everything else seem beside the point. The smile
overrode every other sensation apart from pleasure.

'No, that's fine, thank you. I've already eaten.
I've still got some more to do tonight, but I came
home to see Isaac before his bedtime.'

Charlotte turned quickly. She wasn't being
fair. He had things to do. He didn't take her for
granted, as Peter had done, expecting his dinner
to be on the table whatever time he came home.

'Coffee, then.' She smiled brightly at him.
'You'll have some coffee? And I made cheesecake.'

'That sounds fantastic.' He caught Isaac's eye.

'Hey, are you having cheesecake, too? Or are you just going to run around the kitchen while I eat?'

Isaac swooped towards the table, flapping his arms like a pair of wings, and sat down next to Edward. For the moment, at least, before Edward retreated again into his study, the world was as it should be.

The operation must have finished hours ago. It was ten o'clock, and Edward still wasn't home. Charlotte had tried his mobile and it went straight to voicemail. She didn't dare try again, because a list of missed calls from her would look as if she was crowding him. There was only one thing to do, and that was call the hospital.

It took a while to pluck up the courage to do it, and then another five minutes of waiting on hold before she got to speak to the right person. Then she wished she hadn't. It was only a twenty-minute drive from the hospital at this time of night, and Edward had left at nine.

'Not to worry. Thanks.' She smiled into the phone, as if that might give some believability to her words. Of course she was going to worry.

'He said he was going to check back in again when he got home... If there's any message?'

Charlotte pursed her lips and then went for it. 'Can you tell me whether he's done that yet? Checked back in?'

'Yes, hold on...' A keyboard clicked into the silence on the line. *'Here it is. Yes, he called in about twenty minutes ago. Said we could reach him on his mobile if there was any problem.'*

'Thanks. I'll try that, then.'

Charlotte hung up. So what was she going to do now? Edward obviously hadn't been in an accident on his way home because he'd called in. And he obviously didn't want anyone to know where he was.

She knew exactly what she *wasn't* going to do. She'd been here before and refused to believe what was staring her right in the face. The cold, hard proof of the credit card statements that her husband had kept hidden for so long. The affair that he had denied for so long. It had almost broken her.

Not again. Edward was a man with secrets, and she wasn't going to sit around, waiting for them to shatter her life. This time she'd protect Isaac— and she'd protect herself.

The following day was a Friday, and he was home early for the first time that week. Last night Charlotte had been unable to sleep until she'd heard the front door close quietly at two a.m. and Edward's footsteps on the stairs, disappearing along the hallway and into his room. She hadn't slept much after that, either, and in the morning Edward had left for the Lighthouse Children's Hospital before she was out of bed.

'I've been thinking.' She'd waited until Isaac was in bed before she spoke with him.

'Yeah?' He looked up from the papers that he was reading.

'I think it's time for Isaac and me to go home.'

He set the papers to one side, blank shock on his face. 'Is there something the matter, Charlotte?'

Everything that she could imagine. Edward was tired of her and didn't know how to tell her. He had another woman somewhere. He was too self-absorbed to really care about her or Isaac. One or more of those, in any combination. Or something else, perhaps, that she hadn't thought about.

'We were only going to stay for a few days. It's been nearly a month and...' She took a deep breath. 'I'm so grateful for everything you've done for us, Edward. But we can't stay on here indefinitely.'

This would be the time for him to say that

they weren't overstaying their welcome. That he wanted her and Isaac to stay. They'd have to talk a bit—about how he seemed to have drawn back recently—but perhaps there was an explanation for that.

He stared at her. 'You want to go?'

Disappointment curled around her heart. 'I think that we should.'

She could see him changing before her eyes. The lover who had turned her world into something that was closely akin to magic was turning into a man. One who accepted her leaving as if it had been inevitable all along and wouldn't say one word to persuade her to stay. Cold grief began to trickle into her heart.

'And us?'

She was almost ready to beg him. She would have done almost anything to keep him just for one more day. One more day when anything might happen, when she might find a way to penetrate the icy shell that seemed to be forming around him. Then she thought of the way she'd worried about him last night. The way Isaac had fought to stay awake so that he could say goodnight to Edward.

'Edward, I have no hold on you. Whatever you

were doing last night is none of my business...'
He opened his mouth and she held up her hand to
stop him from speaking. 'No. Really, I don't want
to know. It can't work between us, and I think it
would be better if we just accepted that.'

He could rage against this. Tell her that she was
crazy—that he'd been called away to some medical emergency and hadn't been able to call her.
At this moment she would have believed lies, excuses—anything. But tomorrow she'd wake up
and hate herself for allowing a man to betray her
again.

He ran his hand through his hair and a few
dark spikes fell back across his forehead. 'Okay.
If that's what you want... I'll help you move back
over the weekend.'

'That's all right. You must have things to do...'

He shook his head. 'No. I brought you here and
I'll take you home.'

She didn't have to say it. He'd heard it before,
and Kathy had just been proved right. *Emotionally unavailable.*

Edward couldn't argue with her. She needed
more than he could give and so did Isaac. Scratch
that. They both *deserved* more than he could give.

If breaking his heart was the only way they were going to get it, then so be it.

He hadn't slept much last night, and more than once he'd gone to the door of his bedroom, ready to march along the hallway, gather her up and bring her back. Plead with her—beg her, even—or make love to her until she changed her mind. But each time the futility of such a course of action had stopped him. She didn't want him.

She clearly didn't believe him when he went out early on Saturday morning, with the excuse of having to go to work. Unable to set his mind to anything, he wandered the busy streets, fed the ducks in Hyde Park and dropped in to one of his favourite restaurants for a solitary meal. By the time he got back, late in the afternoon, she had packed hers and Isaac's things and explained to the boy that they were going back home.

Then it was time for them to leave. They somehow managed to stay civil with each other, for Isaac's sake, but they were like actors in a soap opera. As soon as the cameras stopped rolling the smiles fell from their faces and there was no emotion, no more to say. Nothing.

He loaded up his car with their bags and they made the short drive to Charlotte's house in silence. She opened the front door and Isaac ran inside, but it seemed from the way that she blocked the doorway that Edward wasn't welcome. He put her bags down on the doorstep and went back to the car to fetch the rest of them.

She called for Isaac and turned towards Edward. 'Thank you. I'm so grateful for everything that you've done for us.'

Yeah, right. And she was showing him just how grateful she was by leaving. Blocking her own doorway as if he was one of the people that he'd protected her from. The words were on the tip of his tongue when he saw a tear, perched in the corner of her eye and ready to fall.

'If there's anything else you need...'

There was no point in even saying it. They'd lost their opportunity of being friends. He'd blown it—hadn't paid enough attention to the woman he'd thought might be the saving of him—and now they had to part. Better now than some time down the line.

She nodded. 'Say thank you to Edward, Isaac.'

He almost couldn't bear this. Charlotte's cold determination was one thing, but Isaac seemed genuinely sad at their parting. He dropped to one knee and the boy flung his arms around his neck.

'Thank you, Edward. I've had a good time.'

'Me, too.'

'Can we come back to see you again?' Isaac turned his questioning gaze up to Edward.

'Yes, of course. Any time you like. But I'm going to be working hard for the next few weeks. We might not see each other for a little while.' Isaac would probably forget all about him in the space of those weeks. He wouldn't make this more difficult for Charlotte than he had to.

Isaac nodded. 'Okay.'

His trusting acceptance of the lie almost made Edward choke, and he hung for dear life onto the thought that at all costs the child should be protected from the mistakes of his elders.

'Thank you.' Charlotte's face was flushed and she was a moment away from tears.

He should go. Her tears didn't make any difference, and the tearing pain in his chest didn't either. Whatever he felt, whatever he did, it wasn't enough. He didn't have it in him to give any more, and more was exactly what she deserved.

'Take care, Charlotte.' He turned on his heel and walked down the front path without looking back.

CHAPTER SEVENTEEN

CHARLOTTE HAD BEEN dreading returning to work, but it seemed that Edward had dropped out of the life of the Hunter Clinic almost as effectively as he'd dropped out of her own. Even when he was there she wasn't part of his patient care team, and she wondered whether he'd had a quiet word with someone to make that happen.

Perhaps it would be a good idea to look for another job. It was going to be awkward, being faced with the possibility of seeing Edward day in and day out. Particularly since this feeling didn't show any signs of going away. If she had to grieve the loss of the man she'd hoped might be everything to her, then she'd rather do it in private.

She made a few calls and managed to get Friday off. She presented herself at an employment agency at nine o'clock that morning, and by ten she'd been interviewed, the consultant had reviewed her CV, and had promised that she'd be able to find her another job easily.

It was the first step. The next step was to go and see Edward's father, explain the situation to him and ask whether he'd take payment for all that he'd done. It might take a while, but she'd pay that debt off even if she couldn't pay the one she owed to Edward.

When she called his office, his secretary said that he was out all day and took a message. On to step three. She hurried home, changed into an old pair of jeans and T-shirt, and went up to Isaac's room. He'd been so good this week, obviously missing the extra space to play and Edward's large, widescreen TV, but he hadn't complained. Isaac was playing with a friend this evening and she wouldn't be picking him up until eight. She had plenty of time to finish off the little treat she had planned for him.

She surveyed the blank wall opposite Isaac's bed. It wasn't Edward's garden or his TV that Isaac missed. Her son was feeling the same way that she was. He missed Edward. The way he played with him, the way they laughed at the same jokes, how he'd been there for him when things got tough.

'Stop it.' She admonished herself as harshly as she could. Every spare moment she'd had for the last week, whenever she'd been alone, she'd spent the time crying. It was time for her to face facts and get on with it. She'd gone into this with her eyes open, knowing full well that a quiet guy with things to hide was going to cause her pain. Now she'd just got what she had asked for.

She looked at her watch. Eight hours before she had to go and pick Isaac up this evening. She'd better get moving. She hurried to her bedroom and pulled the box of paints and the carefully cut stencils out from under the bed. Time to get to work.

Edward didn't need to think too hard about what he was about to do. He'd already thought it to death, and the one thing he needed to do now was to act. His diary was clear for the day, and he'd hoped that he could make some progress on the research paper that he was writing, but when he'd heard that Charlotte had taken the day off he'd grasped his opportunity.

When he drew up outside her house he noticed that the front window was open. She must be home. He knew that she wouldn't go out without locking the place up securely.

He pressed the doorbell. Flipped the letterbox

open and heard the sound of music coming from somewhere. Looking upwards, he thought he saw some movement behind the thick muslin curtains that shaded what must be her bedroom.

'Charlotte…' He called through the letterbox and waited.

Nothing. The music seemed to have stopped and the house was quiet. He slipped the package he'd brought through the letterbox. That was hers, and if she wouldn't let him in he could at least make sure she got it.

The first part of his plan was achieved. The second would be a little more difficult. He straightened up, wondering whether he should go and wait in his car. She had to come out sooner or later.

His gaze lit on a small arched alleyway which ran between Charlotte's house and next door's, giving access to the back gardens. At the far end were two gates, the one on Charlotte's side slightly ajar.

The gate opened into a small, neat garden. There was washing on the line, and when Edward twisted the handle of the back door it opened.

'Charlotte?' He poked his head inside and called

to her, not wanting to frighten her. 'Charlotte, it's Edward.'

'Go away. Please.' Her voice sounded strained and insistent.

Maybe she was upstairs with someone. Another man, perhaps. Edward shook his head. He knew her better than that.

'Charlotte, I want to speak to you.'

Silence.

'I'm coming upstairs, Charlotte.' He called up the stairs and in the absence of an answer kept walking. He could hear the muffled sounds of movement now, coming from the bedroom at the back of the house.

The door was closed and he knocked, left it a moment and then twisted the handle. The first thing he saw was the plastic taped onto the carpet along one wall. There were pots of paint on the floor, and the start of what looked like a mural on the wall—a giraffe which grinned towards the bed. Then his heart lurched. Charlotte was sitting cross-legged on the floor, in the corner of the room, crying.

'Charlotte. Please don't cry. I only want to talk to you.' He knelt in front of her, afraid to touch her.

She raised her face towards him. Stained with

tears and flushed with defiance. 'So much that you broke into my house to do it?'

'Well, technically I didn't break in. The back door was open.'

'Edward!' Her cheeks bloomed a shade redder and she jumped to her feet, almost knocking him backwards. 'It doesn't matter. I want you to go.'

He stood slowly. He needed a moment to debate what to do next, but she wasn't going to give it to him.

'Just go!' Her outstretched arm pointed the way for him.

'No.'

'I could call the police. You told me that.'

'Fair enough. It's your right to do that. But I'm asking you not to.'

'Why should I listen? You're not listening to what I'm saying.'

'Because I love you, Charlotte.' He'd blurted the words out without thinking. He stepped forward until he was almost touching her, but his head was cool now. 'I love you.'

'Don't!' She dissolved into tears, sobs racking her body. 'Stop it…'

'Can't do that.' He had to go through with it

now, because after this he sure as hell wasn't going to get another chance. 'Won't do it.'

'I can't trust you, Edward.'

'You mean you can't trust anyone. You just can't let go, can you? You might just as well still be married to that husband of yours.'

One sharp intake of breath and she raised her hand and slapped him. Edward had never been slapped by a woman before, and he'd underestimated how much it would sting.

'That might be construed as assault.'

Her hand had flown to her mouth in horror at what she'd done, but she still wouldn't back down. 'You're in my space. I'm just defending myself...'

'I know. You don't need to, Charlotte.'

'What do you know about it?' She pushed him away. 'He did nothing but lie to me—all the time. He told me that he was working when he was out spending every last penny, putting us in debt. He had a mistress and I never even knew about it until their child was three years old...' Tears were beginning to streak her face.

'And you gave him the benefit of the doubt and believed him.'

'Yes. And I'm never going to do that again...'

'Then we're done, Charlotte.'

Edward had never seen himself as a gambler. He weighed up the chances, took the safest route. He'd never before staked everything on one precarious throw of the dice.

Her nerve broke first. 'All right, then. So where were you that night when you didn't come home until two in the morning? Don't tell me you were at the hospital, because I know you weren't.'

'How do you know that?' The old guilt pushed back into his heart. Why did no one ever seem to understand that he needed to be alone sometimes?

'Because I phoned there. You left at nine and said you were going home.'

'I had some work to do at the clinic and I popped in there…' Edward shook his head. This was never going to work on lies. However much he was ashamed of the truth, it was that or nothing now.

He'd had a taste of nothing, and he didn't want to go back to it.

'I went to the clinic and took a swim. Then I went out for something to eat and…just walked for a while. Sometimes I need to regroup.'

She stared at him. 'What's so bad about that? That you couldn't just tell me?'

Suddenly the room seemed too small. Even with

the windows open the pressure of their emotions was intolerable. But he couldn't leave. Mustn't leave. If he did that then he would only prove that he couldn't fight for her.

He took a deep breath. He'd start from the beginning and he'd get it right this time. 'When Kathy left me she said I was emotionally unavailable. That's stayed with me, and I let you go because I didn't believe that I had any right to ask you to stay. I was never sure that I could give you and Isaac the commitment that you both need.'

She opened her mouth to protest and he brushed his finger across her lips.

'Please. I have to say this. I'm older now, and a bit wiser. I know that I can change, and it's time for me to do just that if I've got any hope of you taking me back.'

She shook her head in disbelief. 'No. Oh, no. You don't need to change. Edward, I see right through you. You have feelings and emotions just like the rest of us. You just need to say what they are—not hide them away in case someone doesn't understand you.'

'I think...that's one of the nicest things you've said to me.' She'd said a lot of nice things, and he couldn't be sure.

'What? That you have feelings…?'

'No, that you see right through me. If you do, then you'll know how much I love you. How happy you make me. That I'll never let you down.'

She stared at him. This was everything she'd ever wanted. All she had to do was take it.

'You have to trust me, Charlotte. You told me once that I could learn. So can you.'

'I…I'm not such a quick study as you…I'm going to be rubbish at this.'

'Fair enough. We can both be rubbish together. Do you believe that I can give you my heart? And that it'll be enough for you and Isaac?'

It felt as if she was making a solemn vow. 'Yes, I do.'

'Well, then it follows that you must trust me.'

She took hold of the end of his tie. Tugged a little. He moved closer. 'We're two sides of a coin, aren't we? Very different.'

'Yeah, but it's the same coin.'

'Back to back?'

That smile that Charlotte loved so much. Sexy, thoughtful, provocative.

'I prefer face to face.' His hands moved to

her waist, and she melted into his warmth. 'Although…'

She stopped him with a look. There was time to talk sex later. This was more important and she couldn't wait any longer to say it. 'I love you.'

'I love you, too, Charlotte.' He glanced around, as if looking for some way to prove it. 'I love you so much that I'll help you finish that mural for Isaac. Even though I'm wearing an Italian silk suit.

'You could go home and change.' But suddenly she didn't want him to go anywhere.

'I won't get that twenty minutes back again.'

She was going to have to get used to feeling this happy. At the moment it was too heady, and she could hardly breathe. 'I could come with you.'

He nodded. 'That's a great start.'

CHAPTER EIGHTEEN

'WHEN DO YOU need to pick Isaac up?' He was carefully putting the finishing touches to his part of the mural.

'Not for another couple of hours. He's gone to play at a friend's house. I have to pick him up at eight.'

'I'll take you, if that's okay. I've missed the little guy.'

'Of course it's okay.' A thought occurred to Charlotte. 'I always wondered...'

'Yeah?'

'Why do you have a child's seat in your car?'

He chuckled. 'I got it for when my sister and her little girl came to stay with my parents. She only used it once. I was going to take it out of the car that weekend, but then it came in handy for Isaac.' He paused, his hand hovering over the last delicate part of a lion's eye. 'What? You thought that I had a child tucked away somewhere?'

'No, not really. I just didn't know. Was it okay for me to ask?'

He chuckled. 'Yep. And, in the interests of complete transparency, there's something I need to know too.'

'Fire away.'

'Why does Isaac call that blue rabbit of his Stinky?'

'Ah. The blue rabbit. I seem to remember he was the one that started everything...'

'That's why I feel such an attachment to him.'

'Well, he was originally called Rabbit.' She grinned at him. 'For obvious reasons. Then Isaac threw him into the pond at the park, and when I'd fished him out again I told Isaac he'd need a good wash because he was really stinky.'

'Ah. Makes me feel so much better to know that there's a logic behind it.'

She laughed. 'Anything else you need to know?'

'Not at the moment. You've got paint on your nose.' He closed the distance between them and swiped at her nose with his finger.

'Better?'

'Not really. I just seem to have smudged it.' He grinned, looping his arms around her waist. In the last few hours all the barriers between them seemed to have disappeared. At some point, while they were painting the bright, colourful mural, all the promises they'd made, the honesty and the trust, had turned from just words into reality.

'Do you think he'll like it?'

'Well, *I* like it.' Edward grinned. 'I think he'll love it. The monkey's great.'

'And your lion. He looks a bit like you.' She pulled at one of the dark spikes of hair that had fallen across Edward's forehead, which mirrored the slightly rakish look of his lion's mane.

He laughed, sweeping his hair back off his forehead with one hand. 'He's more like you.' Edward kissed her eyelids. 'Golden eyes...' he loosed her hair from its bonds at the back of her head, smoothing it over her shoulders '...golden hair...'

'A nasty roar...?'

'That's one of the things I love about you.'

'What else?'

'Let's get cleaned up. Then I'll tell you.' He backed out of Isaac's room, pulling her along the hallway. 'You'll have to hurry. There's a lot to get through.'

They showered together, his strong, gentle hands soaping her clean as if they were washing away what had gone before, starting again. Then they made love. As if it were possible to actually create and mould love into the shape and texture that fitted both their hearts, feeling it grow and flourish between them.

Charlotte had wondered whether there could be anything better than the slow, almost silent build of heat that Edward gently nurtured until the fire in him broke loose and roared through them both. Now she knew. When he told her everything that he was feeling her heart spoke back, sharing the warmth, sharing the longing. Body and soul. He made love to her body and her soul.

They lay together, perfect and still, a fine sheen of sweat covering their bodies. Even that seemed to be something shared...his scent covering her skin. She knew that she was never going to be able to wash it off.

'It'll be time to go soon.' He smoothed a strand of hair back from her face. 'However much I want to see whether next time can be as good as the last.'

'Hmm... Me, too. Will you stay for something to eat tonight? Isaac would love to have you read a bedtime story for him.'

'I'd love that, too.' A thought seemed to occur

to him. 'What did you do with the packet that I put through your letterbox?'

'The one with your father's practice logo on it? I thought that came in the post?'

'No, I left it there.' He grinned at her. 'Go and get it.'

Edward knew that she'd torn the wrappings from the parcel as she walked back up the stairs because he heard her gasp of surprise. She walked back into the bedroom, tears streaming down her face and her mother's ruby necklace in her hand.

'Edward. Where did you get this?'

'Put it on and I'll tell you.'

Her hand flew to the neck of her silky dressing gown. 'I'm not really dressed for it.'

'Then take that off.'

She laughed, jumping onto the bed and handing him the necklace to fasten around her neck. 'So tell me where you got this.'

'I had help. You put my father in touch with the guy you sold it to. Luckily he keeps good records, so he was able to forward our letter on to the woman he'd sold it to.'

'And…she sold it back to you?'

'Well, I didn't break into her house and steal it,

if that's what you're worried about. I told her how much I wanted it, and why, and she sold it to me. And now it's back where it belongs.'

'Edward… It must have cost you…'

He silenced her. 'I wanted to undo what's been done. Give you some reason to trust.'

Her eyes filled with tears. 'You're the only reason I need.' She clasped her hand to her neck. 'I love that you've done this for me, but I don't need anything other than you.'

'You have me.' He held her close, revelling in the sound of her heart beating beneath the thin fabric of her dressing gown. 'There's nothing to stop me from giving you more, is there?'

'But I have nothing to give you in return.'

'You and Isaac have already given me everything I'd ever want. More than I ever thought I could have. But there is something you can do for me.'

He wondered whether he should really ask this of her. Charlotte had said she trusted him, and he believed her, but perhaps this wasn't the time to be testing that out.

'What is it?'

'There's something I have to do tomorrow and I can't tell you about it. That'll be the last time you don't know where I am.' He watched her intently, looking for any signs of suspicion in her eyes.

She took his hand and laid it over her heart. Then kissed him. The taste of happiness, right there on his lips. 'I'll see you on Sunday, then.'

'You can rely on it. Eleven o'clock.'

At five to eleven on Sunday morning Isaac jumped down from his perch at the sitting room window and thundered into the hallway. 'He's here...'

'Open the door, then.' One last look in the mirror at her hair and make-up, and the pretty white top that she'd splashed out on yesterday, and Charlotte hurried downstairs to find Isaac and Edward deep in conversation in the hallway.

His smile, when he caught sight of her, told her everything she needed to know.

'You look gorgeous.'

'Thank you. You look pretty gorgeous yourself.'

Edward grinned, pressing on with what was clearly a well-planned preliminary to their afternoon. 'I've just been asking Isaac, as the man of the house...' he glanced conspiratorially at Isaac '...whether it's all right to kiss you.'

Charlotte could feel the happiness radiating from her. 'And what did he say?'

'I said yes. That will be quite all right.' Isaac seemed to be taking his duties seriously.

'Good.' She grinned at Edward and he took a step forward, kissing her lightly on the lips.

'Is that all?' Isaac sounded disappointed.

'You think I should kiss her a bit more?'

'Yes.'

Edward took the hint. Taking her in his arms, he bent her backwards until she would have slipped over if he hadn't had her safe in his embrace. He kissed her on the lips until she was dizzy.

'Better?' He set her back on her feet.

'Much,' Charlotte whispered into his ear.

'Yes.' Isaac gave his blessing to the proceedings. 'Can we go now? I want to fly my kite.'

Edward laughed. 'That's all part of the plan.'

They drove to the same spot where they'd flown their kites the last time, carrying their bags up the steep slope to the summit. Laying a rug out on the grass, Edward opened the picnic basket she'd prepared, inspecting its contents.

'Strawberries?' He grinned up at her.

'Yes. And I've saved some more for later. When Isaac's in bed.' She grinned back at him.

'That I like the sound of. Come here.'

They sat together in the sun, watching Isaac,

who was running around in circles, emulating one of the gliders they'd seen in the sky.

'I still can't believe it.'

'What can't you believe?'

'That you're here. That I love you so much.' She shifted into the circle of his arms. 'You and Isaac. I don't think I could ask for anything more than the both of you.'

'Shame. You won't be wanting any of this, then.' He reached for the cool bag he'd brought and drew a bottle of chilled champagne out of it.

She chuckled. 'Well, maybe just a glass. But won't it be a waste? You won't be able to finish the rest; you're driving.'

He shrugged. 'We can finish it when we get home.'

The cork popped out of the neck of the bottle and flew spectacularly through the air. Isaac's head followed its trajectory and he ran to pick it up, stowing it in his pocket before resuming his imaginary flight up and down on the grass.

Edward turned towards her, handing her a glass, his own only half full. She tipped hers against his, smiling. 'To today.'

'And all the others to come.'

'Yes.'

She took a sip, aware that he was watching her intently. 'This is nice.'

He nodded. Took a sip from his own glass, never taking his eyes off her.

'What?'

'You're so beautiful.'

He made her feel beautiful. She leaned forward and kissed him.

'I love you, Charlotte. You and Isaac.' His gaze was still on her, dark and intent. 'You've shown me how to live my life, and I won't let you down.'

He seemed to have something on his mind. 'What's the matter, Edward?'

'Drink your champagne.'

She lifted the glass, and as she tipped it something solid slid against her lips. Jumping, she emptied the glass onto the grass beside her. 'What was that?'

Edward started to chuckle, flopping onto his back on the blanket, as she searched in the grass.

'Don't laugh—there was something in my drink...' She searched in the grass to find whatever it was, and then she saw it. Sparkling in the sunlight.

'That didn't go quite the way I planned.' He was still lying on his back, laughing.

'Did you put this in my glass?' She leaned over him, holding the ring in front of his nose.

'Yep. I thought it might be romantic. You know—finding a ring in your glass. But you weren't looking at what you were drinking.'

'That's because I only have eyes for you.'

He chuckled. 'Clearly.' He wrapped his arms around her and she leaned in for a kiss. 'So now that I've messed that up completely...'

'No, you haven't. You couldn't have done anything nicer.'

'Well, will you? Marry me? I meant everything I said, Charlotte. About loving you and looking after you and Isaac...'

'I know. I love you, too, Edward. And, yes, I'll marry you.' She handed him the ring, wanting more than anything for him to slip it onto her finger. 'Was this what you were doing yesterday?'

'Mmm-hmm. Do you like it?'

'It's perfect.'

She looked at the ring in his hand. Three large diamonds. One for each of them—the family that she'd so wanted. Her heart was going to burst if things got any better.

Isaac skidded to a halt next to Edward and flung himself across his stomach.

'*Ooof.* Steady on, mate, I was just having a conversation with your mother.'

'What about?'

Edward laughed, giving in to the inevitable. Heaving himself upright, taking both her and Isaac with him, he held the ring up for Isaac to see. 'I've asked her to marry me.'

'Do you love her, then?'

Charlotte smiled. Isaac seemed instinctively to know the only thing that mattered.

'Yes, I do.'

'Does she love you back?'

'Yep. I think she's crazy, but she loves me.'

Isaac looked from Edward to Charlotte and then back again. 'Will we come to live with you?'

'What do you think about that?'

'Can I have animals on my wall? At your house?'

Edward chuckled. 'Well, it'll be *our* house if you come to live there. And you can definitely have animals on your wall. I'll paint them for you myself.'

'Okay.'

Isaac watched as Edward slipped the ring onto her finger. It fitted perfectly.

'Well, that's a relief.'

His smile said it all. Charlotte wanted to see that smile for the rest of her life.

'Are you going to kiss her again?' Isaac was clearly interested in doing things properly.

'You know what, mate? I think I just might.'

* * * * *